Rise Of The Snow Queen

Book Four:

The Frozen Heart

A Winter's War

Mullins

LIGHT OF THE MOON
PUBLISHING

ISBN: 978-1-958221-29-7

First Printing

This is a work of fiction. Names, characters, businesses, places, events, and incidents are either the products of the author's imagination or used in a fictitious manner. Any resemblance to actual persons, living or dead, or actual events is purely coincidental.

Light Of The Moon Publishing has allowed this work to remain exactly as the author intended, verbatim, without editorial input.

Printed in the United States of America

For books available from G.W. Mullins in
Hardback, Paperback and eBook

Visit: https://gwmullins.wixsite.com/books

Or scan the QR Code below

Links to G.W. Mullins pages are on Linktree
https://linktr.ee/gw.mullins

What begins as a simple, bittersweet tale about a man turned into a polar bear, grandly unfolds into a rich, mythical adventure, in this best-selling book series.

Based on Hans Christian Andersen's fairy tale, author G.W. Mullins expands on this classic story creating a new mythology that takes readers into the land of snow and ice.

Rise Of The Snow Queen
Book Series

The Polar Bear King   War Of The Witches   The Story of Gerda and Kai

The Frozen Heart

Rise Of The Snow Queen Series

What begins as a simple, bittersweet tale about a
man turned into a polar bear, grandly unfolds into a
rich, mythical adventure in this best-selling book
series.

Based on Hans Christian Andersen's fairy tale,
author G.W. Mullins expands on this story creating
a new mythology that takes readers into the world
of snow and ice.

Long before the adventures of Gerda and Kai, this
story takes readers to a remote mountain village,
where Winter claims lives, at the Snow Queen's
command. The story goes back to the Mirror and
how it cracked, sending its shards into the world to
infect the innocent.

This reimagining embarks on a much more adult
tone with the mood turning rather sinister, as the
Snow Queen battles to obtain the mirror. The story
will capture and pull you in as Gerda and Kai make
their appearances by the third book in the series.

Rise Of The Snow Queen Series

Book One: The Polar Bear King
Book Two: The War Of The Witches
Book Three: The Story Of Gerda And Kai

From
The
Dead
Of
Night
Book Series
Death is only the beginning.
Daniel walked in the land of the Dead.
Now the Dead want him back
Daniel Is Waiting
Daniel Returns
Daniel Awakens
Daniel's Fate
G.W. Mullins

From the Dead Of Night Series

Death Is Only The Beginning. Daniel walked into the land of the dead. Now the dead want him back!

Daniel Stratton died in a tragic accident. His life should have been over, but it was not. His spirit spent the next sixty years trying to communicate with the people who came to the cemetery. Then, Jen came one night to the mausoleum, seeking refuge from a life that was spinning out of control. It was there she found Daniel.

As they work to free him from the cemetery; they learn that the Light comes for all dead, Daniel is forced to enter it. Inside he sees seven Shadow People within the light, and each one marks him. Daniel knows these Shadows will come for him. Each one in the body of a human who has just died. To survive, Daniel and Jen must escape the "Shadows" that are coming for them.

From the Dead Of Night Series

Book One: Daniel Is Waiting

Book Two: Daniel Returns

Book Three Daniel Awakens

Book Four: Daniel's Fate

Messages From The Other Side Series

Best-selling author G.W. Mullins shares his personal journey toward understanding death, the afterlife, and communication with the spirits of loved ones who have passed over. In "Messages From The Other Side Stories of the Dead, Their Communication, and Unfinished Business," Mullins tells of dealing with the grief of his mother's passing and the reassurance of an after-death communication that changed his outlook towards death and grief.

This book not only tells of Mullins' personal journey into understanding but also guides others to understand why we receive communications and the signs to look for. Mullins also explores visitation dreams and tells of his own experience in the area and shares the stories of others who have had similar experiences.

This book highlights the author's journey in an exploration for knowledge, and his understanding that, without question, there is life after death.

**Messages From The Other Side Series**

Book One: Messages From The Other Side

Book Two: Crossing Over

In order to save his uncle, Malachi is forced to summon Santa Muerte, the deity of death. With his soul on the line, he must do her bidding, to regain his freedom.

To fight evil, you have to embrace the darkness

Rise Of The DarkLighter

From Best-Selling Author

G.W. Mullins

Dark Awakening
Night Of The Demon
Available in Hardback, Paperback and eBook

Rise Of The Dark Lighter Series

Mullins returns to the familiar world he created for the "From The Dead Of Night" series while building a new story in this universe. In the book "Daniel's Fate," Mullins left his audience with an ending that promised more. In this latest book, he delivers, with a continuation of the final battle between good and evil.

To save his uncle, Malachi is forced to summon Santa Muerte, the deity of death. He offers a year of his life in exchange for her help. With his soul on the line, he must do her bidding, to regain his freedom.

The dead begin to rise, as Angels and Demons prepare to wage war for control of humanity. Malachi must choose a side as Armageddon begins.

"Dark Awakening" is the first of three books from "Rise Of The Dark Lighter." This new series is a continuation of his "From The Dead Of Night" books.

Rise Of The DarkLighter

Book One: Dark Awakening

Book Two: Night Of The Demon

Danni liked the quiet upstate New York house she had moved to...
Until she realized something else was living in the house with her.

VENGEANCE

SOMETIMES
THE THINGS YOU CANNOT SEE,
CAN BE THE MOST DEADLY.

Available worldwide in Hardback, Paperback and eBook

G.W.
Mullins

Vengeance
A Paranormal Murder Mystery

*"Mystery, Murder, Paranormal Events, and a story
that leaves you guessing as the bodies stack up."
– Matthew Trent OutLoud Magazine*

After the death of her father, Danni starts a new life
in a seaside town in New York where she and her
mother move into a strange Gothic house with a
terrible history. From the moment Danni gets there,
she feels she is being watched. She is sure they are
not alone in the house.

As Danni learns of her new home, she is told of a
past resident who fell to her death on the nearby
cliffs at the same time that her teenage daughter,
Elizabeth, disappeared.

Elizabeth's spirit appears to Danni and claims that
her mother's death was a murder, not suicide, and
asks for Danni's help in bringing the dangerous
killer to justice.

The mystery unfolds as Danni enlists the help of the
hunky new friend she has made named Joe. A
romance develops between them, but does Joe know
more about the murder and disappearance than he is
letting on? Will Danni live to solve the murder?

As the city darkens and humans descend into sleep, a powerful entity known as the Sand Man, takes control of our dreams and nightmares.
DREAM WALKER
Don't Fall Asleep, The SandMan Is Coming!
DREAM WALKER
ENTER THE SANDMAN
G.W. MULLINS
DREAM WALKER
WIDE AWAKE IN DREAMLAND
G.W. MULLINS
Enter The SandMan
Wide Awake In Dreamland
Available in Hardback, Paperback and eBook
G.W. Mullins

Dream Walker Series

They say a dream is a wish, but what they forgot to mention, nightmares are dreams too. As the city darkens and humans descend into sleep, a powerful being enters the Earth Realm. This mysterious creature, known as the Sandman, takes control of our dreams and battles for control of our souls.

After a boy named Zach is taken into the other realm, he awakens to a new world filled with nightmares. He is joined by two others, Daniel and Jen, as they battle to escape the Dream World and find their way back to reality. Beware the Sandman is coming.

"Enter The Sandman" is the first of three books from Author G.W. Mullins' "Dream Walker" book series. This new series shares a couple of familiar faces from the Best-Selling "From The Dead Of Night" books, featuring the Best-Selling titles "Daniel Is Waiting" and "Daniel Returns."

Dream Walker Series

Book One: Enter The SandMan

Book Two: Wide Awake In Dreamland

Nick Grainger
Book One
The Curse Of Cleopatra
G.W.
Mullins

Nick Grainger Series

Building on the concept that the Earth was once populated by a superior Ancient Alien race, this new book series takes the reader on an adventure through gateways to the multiverse.

Nick Grainger, a young college student working on an archaeological dig in Egypt, accidentally activates a gate to a different universe. He along with three of his companions, are thrown into the ancient alien gateway system between parallel worlds. Lost in the multiverse, they must search for a way home.

On their journey, their gate opens into strange new worlds, similar to their Earth, but in different times and in places. It is on one such Earth, they arrive in Egypt, not as it was in the days of the ancients. Now, it is a place where a technologically advanced race of gods rule.

These new gods of Egypt live through taking the bodies of human hosts. It is there, that Nick must fight his ultimate battle, as he is designated to be host to the god Anubis.

"Nick Grainger The Curse Of Cleopatra" is the first of three books from Author G.W. Mullins' "Nick Grainger" book series.

FROM THE AUTHOR OF "RISE OF THE SNOW QUEEN - THE POLAR BEAR KING" AND "DANIEL IS WAITING"
THE LEGEND OF WHITE BEAR
Extended Edition
EVERYONE HAS A BEAST WITHIN THEM...
G.W. MULLINS

The Legend Of White Bear (Extended Edition)

Nita's tribe faced the coming of the bear every full moon. When it came, many would die.

To protect his daughter, the chief sent her away to live in a rip in time and space, called the void. He told her it was for her protection, but he never told her of the bear's history.

One member of his tribe was burdened with carrying the bear shapeshifter trait. For a lifetime, they would be cursed with being both human and bear until their death. Then a new child would be born to carry the trait.

While in the void, Nita discovers the true horrifying history of the white bear.

THE CONVERGENCE
BOOK ZERO
MASS DESTRUCTION
WELCOME TO THE BEGINNING OF THE END
From the Author of the Best-Selling Book Series "Dream Walker." Inspired by the artwork of C.L. Hause.
G.W. Mullins

The Convergence Series

In the year 2029, the third world war will begin. After the global population is pushed to the brink of insanity from the recent pandemic, they plunge into hatred and violence. With the space race to colonize the moon, man seeks a refuge from the insanity, and the impending environmental destruction brought on by decades of pollution.

In the worldwide confusion, the inevitable happens, when a single nuclear warhead is fired by the command of an insane dictator. Nuclear retaliations are sent forward, ending in the destruction of the Earth's moon. The end of mankind as we know will begin. Human civilization is cast in ruin. A strange new world rises from the old; a world of mutation, super science, and magic. Witness the Convergence. The countdown begins now.

The Convergence Series

Book Zero: Mass Destruction

Book One: Armageddon

Other titles available from G.W. Mullins include:

Timeless - An Adult Paranormal Romance Novel

Aliens, Gods, And Other Paranormal Native American Tales

The Native American Story Book Volume 1-5- Stories Of The American Indians For Children

Walking With Spirits Volumes 1-6 Native American Myths, Legends, And Folklore

The Native American Cookbook

Star People, Sky Gods, And Other Tales of The Native American Indians

More Star People, Sky Gods, and Other Paranormal Tales Of The Native American Indians

For Clarence

"Even the strongest of bonds can become frostbitten and frozen, if not nurtured."

The Snow Queen

"It is only the hearts of the pure that can melt the winter's icy grip."
The Snow Queen - **Hans Christian Andersen**

"It is only the hearts of the pure that can melt the winter's icy grip."

Included at the end of this book, are the first chapters of G.W. Mullins' Best-Selling Series "The Convergence" Book Zero "Mass Destruction"

The following book and the others included in this series are loosely based on folktales. The stories are mainly from Denmark and Norwegian lore. Some aspects are based on the original stories while other parts have been expanded and added to. This four-part series is meant to take the series and expand it to an epic tale.

"Gerda, don't you know what you are capable of?"
The Snow Queen - **Hans Christian Andersen**

An excerpt from

Rise Of The Snow Queen Book One

The Polar Bear King

Before

Jorgen gathered his climbing gear for early the next morning. He was determined to make his way to the mountain before the storm that was due later in the week. As he packed, his son Kristoffer watched intently, his eyes were filled with wonder and dreams of the climb. He wanted so badly to be at his father's side as he reached the top of the mountain.

"Papa, I want to go this year. I have practiced, I wouldn't be in your way." The boy pleaded.

"Kristoffer you are only nine. You would not be able to climb the rocks and hold the ropes as I do. I have told you many times when you are older, I will take you." Jorgen looked deep into his son's eyes and saw the hurt, but he knew there was no way he could take him. "Now off to bed with you, it is past your time, and your mother will blame me for keeping you so late.

Jorgen ushered the boy to bed and then looked in on his daughter who slept in the next room. Gerda was sound asleep; she had no desire to climb mountains. Her life was filled with books and learning. He walked over to her bed and leaned in to kiss her on the forehead. She just curled up tighter and clung to her blanket. The fire in the house provided a barrier to the frozen valley around them, but when the wind blew, you could feel the house's every crack.

"Jorgen if you keep watching your daughter sleep, you will never get any sleep yourself," Freya whispered smiling at her husband.

"I know, sometimes I can't help myself, she reminds me so much of you. She'll break hearts one day, just like you did."

"I never set out to break hearts; I just captured the one I wanted. Now, if only I could convince you to stay home tomorrow. I don't want you to go." She lowered her eyes so Jorgen could not see her pain.

"Freya, I have climbed so many mountains. I will be fine, you'll see."

Jorgen checked the house and made sure the fire would last as he headed to bed. Freya watched, unable to speak of the real feelings she had inside. She bore a secret that she dared not tell anyone not even her husband. She knew what was at the top of the mountain, but telling him might open up a bigger, more destructive secret. Silence was her only option for now and a hope he would not be able to reach the mountain peak or find the castle.

Freya did not sleep the entire night, she just lay there and watched Jorgen. She loved him more than anyone she had ever known. He was her family before the children came along. She had tried so hard to leave behind her birth family. Only her sisters remained, and she wanted nothing to do with them.

It had been nearly a decade since she left the mountaintop and renounced her powers. She ran it all through her head over and over again. There had to be some fragment of her abilities left that could protect him on his journey. If she could only keep him from harm, she would use the power again. As she looked over at the bedside table, she saw the broach. Her mother had given it to her as a girl. She treasured it; being it was the only part of her past she allowed to remain.

As she held it in her hands, she ran her fingers over the rose flower shapes that made up its intricate design. "This will have to do." She whispered. Waving a hand over it, the familiar tingling ran through her fingers. A warm glow extended from her hand and engulfed the broach.

The light was bright and red in color, but it did not awaken Jorgen. She smiled as she realized the power was still within her.

As Freya watched the power fill the broach, she whispered a spell of protection. It was then she knew, she had accomplished her goal. Freya quietly slipped out of bed and went down to where her husband had left his equipment. As she looked it over, she saw the side pouch of his pack. It was there she hid his protector. She turned her head upwards, "Mother I promised I would never part with this, but I have to be sure he is safe. If you are watching, please make sure he comes back safely."

The morning came just as Freya finished her mission. She knew Jorgen would be up and leaving soon. As she went to the kitchen to prepare his food, her heart ached. This was wrong and she knew letting him leave, would not result in anything good. Freya also knew she would not be able to stop him. When he made his mind up to do something, it could not be changed. This was the first time she wished she could.

Jorgen came down and ate as he watched Freya. He knew she was troubled, but she would never tell him. He smiled at her as she walked past. As he extended a hand, she took it and looked him in the eyes. "I'll be all right." He tried to reassure her. It didn't work; she knew all too well how dangerous it was to go near the castle.

Jorgen started to leave for his climb when the sun was just up enough to see. He kissed Freya and waved goodbye. As he started his climb, he never looked back. His mission was to reach the top of the mountain before evening. He took the rugged rocks quickly and showed how his years of climbing made him an expert.

Stopping along the way to rest, he would look back and survey the valley below. More than once he was sure he saw something behind him, but after several hours he put it out of his mind. Maybe it was the altitude playing tricks with his mind. He stopped looking back by the afternoon, as he got to the high peaks. If he had looked back again, he might have seen his son Kristoffer making his way just minutes behind his father. The boy had been right; he was able to handle the climb.

The evening came and Jorgen reached the top of the mountain. He looked around him to take satisfaction in his accomplishment. It was then he saw it in the distance; a large structure of sleek and shimmering ice. It was a castle hidden at the very peak of the mountain, not visible to the valley below. He studied it as he walked the slope that led to the entrance.

The outside looked like an architectural dream. The walls surrounding the grounds were flawless. The gate was carved ice as if done by a true craftsman. As he touched the gate it swung open effortlessly. Jorgen was hesitant about entering, he did not want to trespass, but he wondered who could live in a castle of ice. No human could exist there. He entered and walked through the middle of the garden. The flowers there were all made of ice resembling perfect delicate sculptures. No two were alike; they all had been carefully constructed to be flawless.

As Jorgen approached the steps to the huge doors that protected the front of the castle, he called out 'hello' but no one answered. He continued to move up to the point that he could knock. As his hand touched the door it swung open. His heart almost stopped from fear of who or what might occupy the castle. His courage was not enough to take him inside. He backed down the steps where he originally came and to the side. Not realizing what he was doing, he stepped on one of the perfect flowers and it shattered.

The sound of the flower shattering rang throughout the mountain like a bell. Jorgen realized what he had done. He had to go in now and apologize. He just didn't know to whom. As he looked around, he did not notice that someone else had already become aware he was there. Far above on a balcony of the frozen castle, Elaida watched. She had created the gardens and the castle. Her eyes looked on, enraged as she watched her unwelcome visitor.

Kristoffer made his way to the gates of the castle, looking on in childlike amazement. He did not know things like this ever existed. He had never been taught it in school or dreamed it possible. He worked his way through the garden, as his father once again approached the door. Jorgen knocked again and when no response came, he stepped inside. Kristoffer was not far behind as he watched his father sit down his pack by the door and walk to the large opening where a crystal-looking staircase and chandelier engulfed the room.

Jorgen looked around at the decorations that adorned the hall. There were eleven statues made of ice that lined the walls. Each one was unique and carved with specific human features. All so lifelike and at the same time too perfect he thought. He had never seen such work in his life.

"Hello, is anyone here?" He called out and waited for an answer.

"And what do we have here?" A voice came from the top of the steps...

"I am sorry for the intrusion. I wanted to apologize for stepping on one of your flowers." Jorgen continued.

As the female walked down the steps Jorgen could see she was a beautiful woman with very white features and a long flowing sheer gown. Her eyes never left him, as she made her way down step by step. A sinister look covered her face. She looked at him as if she was a wild animal and he was her prey. She stopped several steps from the bottom landing. Elaida liked to be above the ones she spoke to; it gave her an air of power. That is also why the castle was located at the highest peak in the area.

"So, you destroyed one of my creations?" Elaida said lowering her head and glaring.

"I didn't mean to; I was backing down the steps and I stepped backward onto one. I am so sorry I know these creations must be time-consuming. They are so beautiful." He smiled at her.

"Oh, you like my work?" She spoke while looking at him with a psychotic expression.

"Yes, I especially like these statues. They are like nothing I have ever seen. How did you get the expressions so perfect?"

"Fear does a lot when someone is modeling for you. They just need motivation." She said as she descended the steps and began to walk in circles around him.

"Why fear? What is there to be afraid of?" He asked.

"Well…me of course. Do you not find me frightening?" Elaida laughed out loud.

"No, you are very beautiful."

"Flattery… that could almost get you forgiven for destroying my work. You are quite a beautiful man. I have captured so many different looks and body types in my work, but never a man built like you. So many muscles and that handsome face. You could almost melt a girl's frozen heart." She spoke as she continued to walk around him running a fingertip over his chest.

"Thank you I appreciate the compliments." Jorgen said uneasily.

"Not so much compliments, mostly me thinking out loud. I could use a new statue. It has been years since anyone made their way up the mountain. You must be quite the climber; the way is so icy and slick. But then it is supposed to be to keep prying eyes out of my castle."

Kristoffer listened intently trying to understand what was going on. The woman frightened him. She did not seem normal. Her skin looked as if it was made of ice. He managed his fear and waited to see what his father did.

"Do you live here alone?" Jorgen asked.

"Yes, I have for decades, since my parents died and my sisters went to their own domains."

"Aren't you lonely?"

"No, I have my friends here to keep me company."

"I am Jorgen, what is your name."

"My family called me Elaida. I have been known by many other names over the years. Maybe you have heard of me by reputation. How does the name Snedronningen strike you?"

"You are the Snow Queen?" he said taking a deep breath.

"Yes, I see you have heard of my bad reputation. People seem to misunderstand me so much; they have labeled me as frozen. I am so much more than that, I am ice and destruction. I am a goddess. And you…are less than that."

Jorgen turned to look at the door. He was ready to run, but it was too late. The Snow Queen raised her hand and the ice entered through his feet.

He couldn't move. Kristoffer looked on in fear at the fate of his father.

"You will be my latest masterpiece. I only had eleven before, now you complete my dozen. So handsome, I might have liked you if my heart was not filled with ice. Now…join my collection."

Jorgen's whole body froze solid as his son watched. In a panic, Kristoffer stood up to run, just as the Snow Queen spotted him. She turned loose a flurry of snow in his direction. Like a swarm of killer bees, they flew in his path like they had a mind and a purpose. As he ran, Kristoffer tripped over his father's pack, and on the ground, fell the broach his mother had put in. He knew what it was and picked it up as he scrambled to the door.

Just outside, the swarm of snow swirled around him. Kristoffer held tight to the broach as the bees touched his skin and piece by piece melted from the warm air that surrounded his body. The Snow Queen watched the magic taking place. "He has been charmed." She screamed. She recognized the broach and a rage soared through her.   Her sister was still alive.

An excerpt from

Rise Of The Snow Queen Book Three
The Story Of Gerda And Kai

Return of the Queen

Gerda held tight to her mother's broach as she curled up into her pillow. The feeling of warmth that it radiated, comforted her. She quickly forgot the snow blowing outside. The frozen city radiated through her room and chilled everything it touched.

It had been a year since her mother's death. Everything in her life had changed since then. Her childhood on the mountain was quickly becoming a memory, one so painful she had begun to hide it deep within. Her life in the city was new, different, and best of all, distracting.

Gerda's dreams were filled with images of her mother's death as if they were trying to force her to accept what had happened. …But this time it was different. The dreams were filled with things she did not witness. She had no memories of the actual event of her mother's death.

The broach, being an instrument of magic, retained the events of the past. It slowly fed them into her brain as she slept, its enchantment was strong. Its power was greater than anyone had believed, more than a young girl would have ever imagined.

As Gerda's head moved back and forth, the visions intensified. It was more than she was ready for. As Gerda threw her head back into the pillow, she stepped into the vision. She gasped, as she saw her mother with a group of witches, all-powerful and ready to defend themselves against the Snow Queen known as Elaida.

The sisters held tight to each other as Freya channeled their powers. She felt the full strength of the sisters, and the feeling turned her stomach. Buried deep in their abilities was a layer of underlying evil. It was too much for her.

The Snow Queen looked on at them in disgust. She had always had a hatred for them since the day her parents died. It was she who killed them, but she blamed it on all those around her. The past flashed in her memories, as she looked into the mirror.

Turning back towards the witches, the Snow Queen flew out of control, as she prepared for another blast. She moved closer to the mirror, drawing on it for the ultimate power, she would need to deal a fatal blow. As she released her wave of channeled energy in the direction of the sisters, Damian appeared between her and her targets.

The Snow Queen gasped in fear at his appearance. He had healed from his injuries. His head was lowered as he looked at her with eyes of fire. She dropped her hands, and the ice she created fell to the floor. She had a more pressing engagement than her sisters. The Prince of Darkness was upon her.

"I warned you if you ever tried to take the mirror, I would turn lose all the demons from hell. Maybe I don't need them…I might enjoy doing this myself." Damian's laughter filled the room as he prepared to strike.

"No!" Freya yelled at him. "You will not kill her. We came with the intention of removing the mirror from her and taking her power. We do not want her dead."

"Ladies, I appreciate your cause, and I agree she should be punished. But this is my battle…not yours. The mirror is mine and I will have it…and her life as well." Damian turned back to the Snow Queen. "Prepare to die."

As Damian unleashed his power, Freya turned to her sisters. "We have to save her. We do not have to like her to be family. Help me."

The sisters each raised their power and once again Freya channeled it, but instead of Elaida, their source was now Damian. As she unleashed the power, Freya found her mark by hitting Damian in his back.

He flew forward as the power engulfed him. Falling to the floor Damian had only one recourse, he turned to Freya and blasted her with the full force from within him. As Freya fell, her hand let go of her sister.

Ragnhild fell to her knees and wrapped her arms around Freya. The other sisters looked on in disbelief. They never anticipated anyone would die. The Snow Queen herself looked on in confusion as her sister lay there on the floor.

She regained herself, and once again pulled on her power as she had before and took aim at Damian. As the sisters took her cue, they used the power of the three remaining sisters to attack him. Damian struggled as he regained his strength and then drew from the mirror what he needed.

"Women, I do not blame you for what has happened here today. This should have never been your fight. You were never meant to be here. For that reason, I will not kill you. You are to go back to where you came from. Each of you to your own realm, with no memory of this event ever happening." Damian breathed deeply, then with a wave of his hand sent the sisters flying through time and space to their lands.

"Now, you are mine." He regained his anger as he turned to find the Snow Queen gone. "Where the hell did you go? You know I will find you eventually." He screamed as he walked to the mirror. "And you…. you have caused quite a lot of trouble. Too much trouble, to allow you to exist. If it was not her, it would be another coming to claim you.

Taking the mirror in both of his hands, he transported them both to the sky above the castle. Climbing higher into the sky he looked to the heavens. "I cannot destroy you, but there is a higher source that can."

As he transcended the clouds, the mirror began to vibrate. The higher it went the more it shook, until he reached the highest point, he had ever dared to fly. It was there the mirror cracked. A fine line of lines ran the whole surface of the glass. As he flew around in a circle the glass shattered completely.

Flying on the winds in all directions, the glass went out to cover the earth below. There were larger pieces and small ones. Some were small shards, while others were microscopic in size. As they landed, they were found by people from all walks of life. Some used the glass for windows, others found pieces the right size for eyeglasses, while others were the victims of the glass, when the small pieces pierced their eyes.

The result was the same, wherever and however the glass was found. The evil within changed the view of the receiver. If they looked through the glass, they saw the worst of the world. If the glass entered a person's body, it would eventually find its way to their heart. They would grow cold and hateful. No matter their true nature they were changed.

Making her way back to the staircase, she looked down to where Freya's body lay on the floor. The lower level was a mess of debris and rubble. Descending the staircase, Elaida could not take her eyes off Freya. Something deep inside her was not right. She felt the pain of loss. Her cold heart did not usually allow this feeling. It was something she did not care for.

As the Snow Queen reached the bottom of the stairs, she fell to her knees next to Freya's lifeless body. She stared down with her icy gaze. Her hatred for her sister was gone. In a brief moment of humanity, emotions overtook her, she felt the pain of her parent's death, and then Freya.

Cradling Freya's body, she rocked back and forth. Holding tight, like she was cradling a child, Elaida screamed out in pain. "What have I done."

She began to cry as she buried her face in Freya's shoulder.

An excerpt from

Rise Of The Snow Queen Book Three
The Story Of Gerda And Kai

The Escape From Fall

Gerda sat up and shook her head. She stood up and dusted the filth from her clothes. She did not believe what she had learned. How could a reindeer talk?

"You are a reindeer?" She asked.

"Yes, and from the little I saw, you are a human." He jokingly replied.

"How is this possible, reindeer do not speak."

"Enchanted reindeer do. That is part of the reason, I am locked away here. The robber girl wanted me because I was special. If I were any other deer, I would have been eaten for dinner. The robber girl is a selfish spoiled brat, and her mother allows her too much. That is the reason I am held captive here." The reindeer explained.

"Do you really know the way north?" Gerda asked.

"Yes, and I so badly want to return there. If I can get free of this place."

"If I freed you, would you lead me to Lapland?" Gerda asked.

"Yes, for my freedom, I would gladly help you on your way."

"Then it is a deal. I will get you free."

"The robber girl will not allow you to take me. She will probably not let you go either." The reindeer called back.

"She will if I play my hand right. By the way, do you have a name?" She asked.

Yes, I am Bae, and you are?"

"I am Gerda, and I am happy to know you."

Gerda and the reindeer talked through the small opening all evening and planned their escape. If the robber girl did not honor their agreement, then Gerda would free herself and Bae, and then leave as fast as they could.

Midnight came, and the robber girl showed up at the door. She had brought food and things Gerda would need on her journey. In the stack, there were boots and gloves. With the addition of Gerda's cloak, she should have enough to stop her from freezing.

"I wish you did not have to go. I would like to have a friend here a little longer at least." The girl said sadly.

"I will come back to be with you again. I just have to go for now. I cannot risk Kai. He has to be freed. Oh, and speaking of freeing, why is the reindeer in the next room?" Gerda tried to be sly about working the question in.

"He is my pet. My mother gave him to me after a raid in the north."

"Would you consider allowing him to travel north with me? He knows the way to Lapland. I do not. I need him to guide and assist me. I would not ask if this was not so important."

"Yes, but none of this will be of any importance if we cannot get you out of here. There are still people awake, and they will see you."

"What if I did not leave on two feet?" Gerda asked.

"What do you mean?" The robber girl was confused.

"Yes, what does she mean? Does she want to ride me like a horse? I am not built like that." Bae screamed out, in his deep-throated voice.

"Quiet, or they will hear you, you fool." The robber girl called out. "Yes, it might work. If you left from the back of the building, you would be hidden, as you got up to speed."

"I just need to get in there with him."

"Stand back," Bae called out as he moved towards the wall and backed up. With a swift kick, and the most of his weight behind it, the inner wall was broken, and a hole opened between them. "Can you get through that?"

"Bae you are a genius," Gerda said through the opening.

As both of the girls climbed through, the robber girl placed her hand on Gerda's shoulder. She smiled at her, as the two hugged. The robber girl acted shy at first but then held on strong.

"You are always my friend, and I will come back to you. I give my word."

The robber girl stood to the side, as Bae allowed Gerda to climb on his back. As they readied to leave, the girl opened the outer door and looked to see if anyone was about. It was clear and she walked back to Gerda.

"Be safe my friend, I will await your return."

Before anyone could see, the reindeer flew out of the building, and tore into the woods, as fast as he could go. Gerda held tight, as they flew through branches and brush. They did not stop until light flakes of snow started to fill the air around them.

"Those are my old Northern Lights!' The reindeer said. "Just look at how they gleam!" Then he shot off even faster, night and day; on their way to Lapland. They both were free and their journey together continued.

An excerpt from
Rise Of The Snow Queen Book Three
The Story Of Gerda And Kai

On the Road to Lapland

As they continued North, the winds blew harder. Bae did his best to carry Gerda into the kingdom, as the sting of the snow-kissed winds, hit him dead on. Neither was prepared, for what lay ahead of them.

"This is not the way I remember this land to be," Bae said, stopping to look around them.

"What do you mean, it is supposed to be winter here, right?"

"Yes, but the winter was not this intense. There is something else going on here. It is her, the Snow Queen. She has changed this place. It was mountainous and snow-covered before. I spent most of my life here, I should know. Now it is hostile and deadly. She made it that way, I am sure."

Gerda climbed down from Bae's back and looked around. It was hard to see much of anything, as the snow blinded her. As she pulled her cloak up to block the snow, she saw on the mountainside, a house that looked as if it could withstand the storm."

"Come, we will take shelter there for a while and rest until we can continue.

Bae agreed, and they headed for the dilapidated building. Gerda held tight to Bae as they trudged their way. The swirling of the wind and snow was disorienting, and more than once, they lost their way.

"It's as if she is playing games with us," Gerda screamed over the sound of the wind gusts.

"I know, I feel it too. I have felt like someone has been watching us for a while now." Bae said as he dragged Gerda forward to the house.

After what seemed like hours, they found the door of the house. It was unlocked and abandoned, but why lock a building, that was falling apart? Gerda rushed through the door with Bae close behind.

"What do you mean, you have sensed we were being watched?" Gerda choked on her words trying to take in the frigid air.

"I am enchanted, as I told you. I have extra senses. I have abilities other reindeer do not. I am from a group of magical creatures." He explained.

"OK, next you are going to tell me you can fly." Gerda sarcastically jabbed at him.

Bae only stood there and cocked his head to the side. He said nothing, for he did not want to reveal all his secrets at once. Gerda stared at him in disbelief. She had never heard of anything like this before.

"How long do we stay here?" Gerda asked.

"I would say until morning. Perhaps by then, the snow will have calmed a bit. Or maybe, she will have gotten bored enough of watching, and then we can make a run for it." Bae said as he shook the snow from his hair.

Gerda looked around and found pieces of wood for a fire. If they were to stay there, she was not going to just sit still and freeze. As she piled the wood into the old rock fireplace, she looked around for a match, but there was none.

Not one to give up, she thought of what the king told her. She inherited her mother's power; she just did not know how to use it. Thinking of the broach's warmth, she held it out to the fireplace and wished for a flame. Nothing happened.

"What are you doing?" Bae asked.

Gerda explained and Bae understood. He was not new to witches or magic. He studied her for a second and being enchanted, he decided a course of action to release her power.

"I am no expert on witches, but you are going about this all wrong. To use your abilities, you have to have intent and purpose for them to execute. You have to want it. Get angry and you may just force it to happen." Bae insisted.

"I am not angry. I am not an angry person."

"Try thinking about the Snow Queen about to kill your friend. That should do it."

Gerda turned back to the fireplace and looked deep into the wood pile. She thought of Kai and she felt a tingling in her hands. The more she thought, the angrier she got. Then her eyes started to glow a reddish-orange color. She had found her power and it was growing.

Gerda let out a scream, as she sent forth a ball of fire into the old fireplace, that exploded so largely, that it shot back and around it as well. Gerda began to laugh as she saw what she had done. She had performed an act of magic.

"You found that funny, huh?" Bae asked.

"No, not so much funny, as a feeling like a dam just burst inside me. I feel different, I feel powerful." She said rubbing her hands together above the fire.

The night went quickly with conversation and the warmth of the fire. As Bae predicted, the morning came, and the wind and snow had died down. As soon as they were ready, Bae and Gerda set out into the deep snow on their way north.

A great distance away, on a mountaintop, stood an ice palace fit for a queen. In that palace, a cold-hearted goddess stood in her great hall. A look of distaste covered her face. The more she watched the snow globe in front of her, the less she was amused.

"So, you survived the night? There are so many other obstacles in your way. I will not allow you to reach Kai. He is mine." The Snow Queen laughed, as she held the snow globe to the light. Inside, the clear image of a girl walking through the snow could be seen. Gerda was on her way and the queen knew it.

Chapter One: My Memories For A Kiss

Kai sat before the mirror looking blindly into it, trying to figure out the Snow Queen's words. He knew her rage. He had suffered it for more years than he could recall. Glancing down at the floor, he tried to sort it all out in his brain, but it was no use. It was as if a mental block stopped him from going past a certain point.

The witch's screams and cursing filled the air of the frozen castle walls. The layers of ice acted as an echo chamber and her words pounded hard in his ears. Kai rocked back and forth on his heels as he shook, looking as if he had become mentally damaged by his captor.

Each word pounded at his head as he tried to block them from entering. Then, he stopped rocking suddenly and swallowed hard. "She did this to me." He whispered under his breath, trying not to be heard. The words left his lips before he could stop them.

The great white polar bear raised his head. He had been deep in meditation, trying to shield himself from the rage the witch unleashed. "She did what to you?" His deep throat growled at the young man, who fell backward before the mirror.

"How long have you been with the queen?" The young man asked.

"More years than I could have ever dreamed possible. More than anyone should have to endure." The bear said with a saddened face.

"And you remember them all?" Kai asked.

"Yes, I am afraid I do."

"Then I am sad for you, but you see, I do not remember. I try, and I try hard. I can remember half my life. Back to the time she came to me…nothing before. I do not know family, friends, or where I am from. The memories were robbed from me."

"I know, and I believe you. It is easier to control someone who has no ties to a prior life. She took your memories. For that, you are lucky. I would have rather had that done to me. Instead, she killed the one I loved, and destroyed everything that meant anything to me." The bear lowered his head trying to hide his sadness.

"And what of your family? Did anyone survive?" Kai asked trying not to upset his only real companion.

"I had a wife and children. My mother is surely long since dead. I had a kingdom which I was to rule after my father's death. I was to take the throne before the queen came to me and changed me into the creature you see before you." The bear turned towards him and his expression changed. "It seems so long ago now. For all I know, everything is gone."

"I am sorry for your loss." Kai tried to comfort the bear, hearing the shaking in the bear's voice. "Do you think you will ever break the enchantment and become a man again?"

"I have given up trying. It has been so long and I have no hope. In my heart, I am still a king. No…now, I am a polar bear king." As he turned to walk away, the sound of his nails on the ice clicked all around him. "If I could become a man again, what would it matter? Everything I loved is gone now. You have more of a chance than I do. Someone out there is still searching for you, and the queen is threatened by her."

Kai looked at the bear as he walked away. He tried to search his brain for a clue as to who could be looking for him. His old life was taken away. No matter how he tried, the memories were behind a locked door. One he knew he could not break through.

Turning back to the mirror, he looked at the broken pieces that had come together to rebuild it.

One piece was still missing. The piece that resided deep within his heart. He did not know what it was at first. The day on the mountain, when the shard of glass flew into his eye. Of all the people on earth who could have received this fatal gift, why him?

He wasn't about to give in to his dread or fear. If the queen wanted the piece of mirror within him, it surely would mean his death. He knew of no other way for her to take it, except to rip it from his chest.

A tear ran down Kai's cheek as he looked hard at the pieced-together glass. The mirror was evil and when it was shattered, it brought too much death and destruction. She brought him there to collect the pieces, and restore the evil so she could use it to rule them all.

He reached out to touch the surface, and a splinter of the glass cut into his flesh. He struggled to breathe as the dark energy flowed into his blood. He was terrified as he heard the voice in his head. "Fear not young one. You are safe from me. I owe you, after all, you have rebuilt me. You have given me life again. For that, I will grant you one desire. Not tainted or dark, but a gift of sight which was taken from you. I will give back what she has stolen."

Chapter Two: Stolen Memories

Kai felt the energy surge through him, as if a dam had burst inside. At first, he was confused, but then it became too clear to him, as his body fell backward to the ice-covered floor. He traveled into the past through his memories. Back to a time when he first came to the castle. This was the point he could never get past, as he tried to remember his life.

Then as he watched for a time, things changed. The images from time swirled around him as a searing pain ran through his brain. He found himself in front of a red door. Inside he heard noises and sounds. He was sure there were people behind the door, but he did not know who.

As he looked down, he saw the keyhole. From within a red light shined out. A swirl of mist floated all around the opening. He was scared and curious at the same time. He feared what might have been inside, but at the same time, he was drawn to it.

Kai moved closer and studied the door. It was nothing special, just a big red door, that held so many secrets. He moved a hand out to touch it, but drew back in fear. "Go on boy, touch it. Take hold of the metal handle and free the spirits locked within. You know you want to." The voice sounded more sinister than ever.

Kai feared whatever was trapped within, but he feared forfeiting his life to the Snow Queen more. He thrust his hand forward and grabbed the handle. The metal was hot, and for a moment burned his hand. "Good boy, she only made it this way to scare you." Kai could hold back no more as he flung the door open.

As the door shot inwards, a cloud of bright light and fog encircled him. As the light closed in and coated his skin, he felt a burning in his brain, as if he was being penetrated by the light. Thousands of images and sounds raced through his brain, too many to process at once. He felt himself falling to his knees, as he gave in to the pain.

Kai passed out, and his mind continued to receive all the memories he had been robbed of. He remembered the city and his home. He remembered Gerda. The shard of the mirror had turned him against her. As he watched, unconscious to the world, his lips moved, as inside he screamed one word. "No!"

Kai's pain ran deep. He could not believe the person he had become, or how easily he was tempted by a stranger. He watched himself go out on the snow-covered streets, leaving Gerda on her own. The mirror brought out the worst in him, turning him into a person he didn't even know. He loved Gerda, how could he have let this happen?

He watched as the Snow Queen tempted him with a new life. She deceived him. He watched as she took him high above the city, and showed him how the snowflakes floated from on high. He heard her words, carried on the air, as if in a dream.

"Come away with me, and your life will never be the same again. You will live in a castle made of ice. Winter will be your playground." The Snow Queen tried to tempt him.

"I have a life here, family and friends. As angry as I have been lately, I couldn't leave Gerda." Kai said as he tried to fight the confusion in his head.

"Gerda could be a memory of the past, something that faded away. You never have to think of her again. I will be everything you need. I could rule with you at my side." She said smiling. "A simple kiss, a suggestion will take all the pain away."

Kai turned away, and looked out of the sleigh. Down on the ground, he studied the people, and snow on the rooftops. His heart struggled to make a choice. How could he leave behind all he knew? The darkness inside, convinced him it was ok. He made his choice.

As he turned to the witch, he smiled a sinister smile. "Will I remember anything?" He asked.

"Not if you do not want to. I will help you forget it all."

As the Snow Queen placed her hand on his shoulder, she pulled him closer and placed her lips on his head. Kai felt a weird sensation, as if he wasn't able to breathe. The world spun around him as he struggled to stay awake. Then, in an instant, he was fine. The pain went away, and he was once again normal.

"Now, do you feel better?" The Snow Queen asked.

"Yes, I am fine." He said sitting up in his seat.

"And what of the girl, Gerda." She asked.

"She will be fine on her own."

Kai relived the memory, as he tried to not scream out. Now he knew what had happened. In the years that passed, she created the door that blocked him. Each year it got stronger, until it was impenetrable to him. He knew then why the Snow Queen was so angry. Gerda had come for him, after all this time. She was still looking for him. As he lay there on the floor by the mirror, a smile made its way across his face.

Chapter Three: Frostbitten

As the light of morning came, it shined through the castle made of ice. The rays of the sun reflected off all the surfaces. It did not melt the objects of reflection; they were too cold and preserved for that. The Snow Queen made sure of it. She put too much time and effort into her work. It was all precisely planned.

Kai sat up as the flicker of light hit his eyes. He wondered what had happened. Had the night before been just a dream. He took a deep breath and tried to remember his past. He was groggy at first, but then he realized it was all there. And still, there was Gerda.

He stood up and moved to the light. It was a reminder of the world outside. He was not allowed to see it anymore. It was because of her, he thought to himself. She knew if he got outside, he would try to run away.

It was not as important that day to worry. He had a secret. He was more himself, than he had been in years. He had his past back. Still, how could he use it to help himself?

As Kai made his way down the frozen hallway, he felt the hunger in his stomach. He was not allowed to eat much. Too much food would give him the energy to fight back. She liked him thin and frail.

Walking past a mirror that covered much of the wall, he looked at his reflection. He was no boy anymore. In the years of his captivity, he had grown into a strikingly handsome man. He could see the features on his face, that reminded him of himself in childhood. Now, he had grown into a tall, but thin man, covered in lean muscle.

He wondered how he stayed muscular, with as little as he ate. Then he realized over the years, he exercised, not by intention, but necessity. When he first arrived, he found ice skates in the castle and used them to fly through the hallways, when no one was around.

He kept his secret exercise well, at first even the bear did not know. Then one day, as Kai flew through the passage at high speed, the bear stepped out into his way and they collided. It was then he realized the bear was to be his protector.

Kai did not understand the bear in the beginning. He did not know that the polar bear was under an enchantment. There was a king inside who was fair and kind. There was a lot Kai did not know in the beginning, like how the Snow Queen was slowly robbing him of his memories and identity. Sometimes, he thought, you learn things the hard way.

Kai searched the grounds. He needed to know where the Queen was. If she was gone, he was safe. Still, he feared she would come back with another piece of the horrible mirror. He was sure there could not be many more, than the one inside his chest. The remaining opening was so small, it was almost microscopic.

"You are safe. She is not here." A voice came from behind him.

"Hello bear. Will she return soon?" Kai called back.

"No, she is occupied by something that is troubling her." The bear replied. "Why do you do that?"

"Do what?" Kai asked.

"When we are alone, you do not have to refer to me as a bear. You know well who and what I am."

"I do it out of fear, not disrespect."

"And how is that?" The bear growled at him.

"If I call you bear all the time, then I will not make a mistake, and call you otherwise in front of her," Kai replied. "If she was aware we had become friends, then she would find a way to hurt one or both of us."

"Point taken." The Bear replied. "I have found food for you. You had better eat, before she comes back and sees I have helped you."

Kai looked at the bear as he began to walk away. He smiled, as he watched the giant of a bear, be so out of character. Kai opened his lips and uttered a thank-you, which made the bear happy.

Kai walked slowly behind as the bear moved through the long hall. He was so full of energy and hope. The hate within him from the mirror, could not overpower his emotions anymore. He was confused by this, but he did not dare say it out loud.

"You are quiet. You always seem to be talking away, or complaining about something." The bear was curious.

"Not today. I awoke rested and calm. Maybe I will not let anything bother me today."

Kai said jokingly, for he knew the queen would not let anyone be peaceful.

"You know where she is, right?" The bear asked.

"Not really, no."

"The girl grows closer to the castle. The queen feels threatened by her for some reason." The bear said as he let out a snort and a huff of breath.

Kai made his way to the frozen table, and began to stuff food into his mouth. He looked up only for a second and studied the bear. He swallowed hard as he thought of a response to the statement. "What makes you think it has anything to do with me?"

"It is the girl, whose mother was the queen's sister. The sister who died. She inherited the broach of power."

Kai looked up, almost choking on his food. He remembered the broach. Gerda had guarded it back when they were children. He could not hide his expression, as the bear turned and looked him in the face. Kai's heart pounded in his chest as he realized the bear knew.

"I thought so, you remember her and the broach." The bear laughed. "I knew something was different. The queen is watching the girl. She fears her. She knows the girl wants you. Be ready young one, a Winter's War is coming, and we are but bystanders in the fallout.

Chapter Four: The Watcher In The Woods

Bae walked ahead of Gerda, as she tried to keep up in the deep snow. She tried hard, but along the way, there were so many things to distract her. She looked on in wonder at the area around her. The snow-covered mountain reminded her of home. Her thoughts immediately went to her father and her grandmother. Then she stopped in her tracks, as she thought of her.

"She must be dead by now," Gerda said out loud not meaning to.

"Who must be dead?" Bae called back.

"My grandmother. She was older when I left to search for Kai. That was so many years ago now. The Spring Witch's spell had me captive for so long. It's just, that I never thought of it before. It just ran through my mind."

Bae turned to look at her, as she ran a hand across her face to catch the tears. Her past had finally caught up to the world she now lived in. She tried to hold back the tears as they ran down her face. The frigid winds blew past her, almost freezing the moisture on her skin. All she could do was fold her arms around her stomach as the wind chilled her to the bone.

Bae came to her side and pushed his nose up close to her. He only wanted to give comfort. She realized his kindness, as she wrapped her arms around his neck and held tight. She clung to him, and his warmth soothed her.

"There are days, I wonder what the hell I was thinking." She tried to speak. "I left everything to run after a boy who pushed me away. In that time, I lost years of my life and my family, all to end up freezing on a mountain to try to rescue someone, who might not even want to come with me. I must be crazy."

"No, my dear, you are in love with a boy, who once showed you love in return," Bae spoke, as he rubbed his cheek against her.

"Maybe he will not know me at all. I was so young when he left. Now I am nearly a decade older." She pulled away, to look him in the eyes. "What horrors could he have been through?"

"Gerda, he has grown and become older just as you have. You were trapped at the hands of a witch, and so was he. You have both suffered. That is not as important, as finding him and setting him free."

"I guess you are right. I just wonder if the worst fight is ahead of us. She will not let go easily." Gerda said as she turned towards the top of the mountain.

"No matter what the case, we stay strong and if we have to, we fight." Bae's words rang out and echoed through the trees of the mountain.

A short distance up above them, a woman walked through the snow. She smiled a sinister smile, as she looked around at the beauty she had created. Leaning over, she reached down to take ahold of a small tree, that was coated in the ice and snow. She studied its branches, as she pursed her lips together and blew in its direction.

The snow from the tree flew into the wind and scattered all about. She took in its elegance, as she expressed the joy it gave her to watch. She tossed the tree to her side as she moved on, swirling through the forest, and sending snowflakes floating from her fingertips.

As she danced, the snow increased and flew upwards into the sky scattering all around the mountain. Gerda looked up as the snow came at her more quickly. She turned to Bae. "She is here, isn't she?"

Bae let out a snort, or something like it, and shook his head. "She is watching us, waiting to see where we go. She is paranoid."

"Why would someone so powerful, be scared of us?" Gerda said as she laughed.

"My dear, you are not powerless, and she knows it. You have your mother's strength and now her magic. We do not know the extent of your abilities."

Gerda looked at him and shook her head. "I feel different, that much is for sure. Do I think I could defeat the Snow Queen? I cannot even imagine it."

"You have something she does not. You are capable of so much love and warmth. It will fuel your fire. You only need to believe."

The Snow Queen made her way down the mountain, continuing to spread snow along her way, until she heard the voices. She stopped for a moment, and then found the direction of the sound. Walking to the edge of the tree line, she saw them from a distance.

"So, there you are my dear, and your sad little reindeer too. Hardly a match for me. So young and beautiful. I was like you once. But time ravages all things. I wonder if he would want you, after the winter ice sends a frostbite all over your face?" The Snow Queen laughed out evilly.

Gerda felt the coldness of the wind which swirled around her. She turned to look at Bae. It felt as if the blast was directed solely at her. She could feel the anger rising inside. The witch was jabbing at her. Gerda was sure she was close by, watching and waiting.

Chapter Five: Reindeer Games

Bae studied the area. He knew where they were. His family had once lived on the mountain. His only wish was to see one of them again. To know safety and warmth, away from the cold that surrounded them.

Bae moved his ears as he heard a noise in the trees. It was the breaking of limbs. He wondered what could be there, whether it be animal or human. He did not want to stay long enough to find out.

The noises came closer and more frequent. He huffed hot air from his nostrils as he contained his urge to charge. Gerda moved in closer, she had heard it too. Someone was closing in on them. She dared not hope it was something innocent. She raised a hand to Bae's back, as her guard went up.

"Why have you come to my mountain?" The voice of the queen morphed, and became harsh with the wind.

"I don't know who you are, but show yourself?" Gerda called out.

"You know who I am, girl. I am the greatest force of winter. I am the source of cold, and death. I am the taker of life. I am the Snow Queen."

"Show yourself!" Gerda screamed.

Out of the trees, the queen emerged. She walked forward like a goddess in the snow-filled air. As she moved from the darkness, the light that came to her skin showed the silvery blue glow, that protected her. The queen's hair was swept back behind her, in frozen layers that looked like shards. As she came closer, her long white gown cascaded down and trailed off in behind.

Gerda stared at her, as she came closer. She had no words; she was mesmerized by the woman-turned-creature, who floated before her. Bae moved around Gerda to take it all in. He moved only a couple of feet before stopping in his tracks. He did not often show fear, but this day he was scared.

Gerda stood her ground, as she searched for the only words she could muster. "Where is Kai?"

"No, No my dear, he is not your concern." The queen said shaking a finger at her.

"He most certainly is my concern. I don't know how you lured him away, but he is coming home with me."

"I don't think that will be possible. You see, you might not even survive this day on the mountain." The queen laughed.

"You wouldn't be the first witch who tried to stop me along the way. I have survived more than one, and even though it has taken me a few years, I am here." Gerda said with confidence.

"If I wanted to, I could freeze you in your tracks. All I would have to do, is call upon the winds."

"If you were going to, you would have by now. We know you have been watching us. And yet, we are still here."

"Gerda, it is not wise to antagonize the one who has the power to unleash winter upon us." Bae insisted.

"I'm done with this. We are moving on, and you will not stop us." Gerda fumed.

"I may not…but I am sure they will." The Snow Queen's voice changed, as she threw her arm to the side. From her hand, a spray of ice and snow, flew over the open terrain. The winds swirled and the snow rose into the air, as large shapes formed.

Gerda watched as they grew. "What has she done?"

Bae watched as he saw the shapes of the polar bears rise onto their hind legs. "Run, Gerda." He shouted as the forms came to life.

"We can't outrun them." She called back.

The bears continued to form, until there were ten in number. Gerda moved back and looked around for any help at all. There was none. She wondered if all she had done was for nothing. She feared death was at her door.

"And now my dear, your journey is over." The Snow Queen had a smile on her face, believing she had won.

"We will not go down without a fight," Bae screamed out.

"Aww, but who will help you?"

"We will defeat you!" Gerda screamed over the growls of the ice-formed polar bears.

"You and what army?" The queen laughed.

"This one!" A voice called out from behind.

As the polar bears flew forward, the sounds of their paws hitting the ground, sounded like thunder. Gerda and Bae turned to see a second army behind them, this one, a group of enchanted reindeer. Bae's eyes lit up, as he saw his family take to the air over their shoulders.

As the bears flew towards them, the reindeer flew high and dived down upon them. One by one they came for the ice bears with sharp hoofs and antlers. The deer flew in hard, and blasted the snow and ice forms to dust, on the ground.

The queen looked on in disbelief. As she watched, she knew she had to retreat, there were too many enchanted creatures for her to manipulate. They numbered more than twenty in all. She turned and took to the woods quickly, before anyone knew she was gone.

"This battle is over," Bae shouted.

"Who are they? Where did they come from?" Gerda could not contain her excitement.

"These, young one, are my family. And I must admit, I have never been happier to see them."

The reindeer gathered around and moved closer. Bae welcomed and thanked them for their assistance. He was happy after so long, and told them his story of imprisonment and how Gerda freed him.

"How did you know we were here?" Bae asked.

"He told us." And older reindeer said, as he motioned to the back of the crowd.

A man came forward with a smile on his face. He was older and dressed in reddish-brown fur. As he came forward, Bae's eyes lit up. He knew the man from when he was a young buck. Bae knew at this point; he was truly home.

"I thought you could use some help." The man said, as he placed the back side of his hand against Bae's cheek.

"Thank you, Nicholas. I am sure you saved our lives." Bae said, with a sound of joy in his voice.

"Yes, but the Snow Queen is not easily controlled. She will come back with a vengeance. Reindeer, take to the skies, we are going home."

Chapter Six: The Land Of Ice And Snow

Gerda leaned over the side of the sleigh, as it flew across the land, before taking to the air. She laughed out loud as she held tight to the sidebars. This sensation was new to her. She had never left the ground before. She wondered if this was a sensation Kai felt, when the Snow Queen took him away.

The airbrushed past Gerda as she felt the snowflakes touch her cheeks. She had not felt so alive in years. She watched as the reindeer pulled the sleigh higher into the clouds. She wondered how many other animals had enchantments.

Turning to Nicholas, she studied his face and his clothes. Something about him was so familiar, but she did not want to be rude and ask. She was grateful to the man who rescued her. No matter who he was.

"You are quiet Gerda," Nicholas said without turning towards her.

"I don't quite know what to say. I am thankful for your rescue. I believed we were about to die."

"Like your mother did, at the hands of the Snow Queen." He said timidly.

"How do you know that? Did you know my mother?" She asked.

"My dear, I know many on this earth. It is my job to know the state of people and their actions." Nicholas answered vaguely.

"You speak in riddles." She said laughing.

"I assure you; I have your best interest at heart. I am a force of good."

"You are a Guardian, aren't you?" Gerda blurted out.

"You didn't hold that back, did you?" He smiled as he answered her. "Yes, I am, and how does a young woman like yourself know of things like that." Nicholas was curious.

"My mother was a witch, a force of good. She was one of the Earth Sisters. That was until the Snow Queen killed my mother, after the sisters tried to contain her."

"So, you know all of what happened?" He asked.

"I have learned some of the story over the years. At least, the years I was not held captive."

"You mean by the Spring Witch?"

"How did you know?" Gerda was puzzled.

"I told you; I observe all. I know the Spring Witch. She is a troubled soul, in need of attention. Since her daughter died, she has sought out a replacement. In her mind, she thinks she is right to abduct someone. I was aware you would encounter her, but at the time I was called away. I only learned of your captivity, after you had escaped. By then it was too late. I did however, allow Bae to come into your life." He said as he looked over to the reindeer flying past him.

"What do you mean? I found Bae being held captive by the Robber Girl."

"I could have saved him long ago, but I knew your paths would cross. You needed him more than I did. So, I allowed him to stay there until you found him." Nicholas reached out his hand, and touched her shoulder. "I helped you, in the only way I knew how at the time.

"You are the Guardian of Winter, aren't you?" Gerda became excited, as she began to figure it out. "That is how you know me; you have been around my whole life, haven't you?"

"Yes, that would be accurate, but humans are not supposed to know of my existence. Only the ones of the magical kingdom, are to have such knowledge."

"I was born to a witch, and when she died, I inherited her power. I am now of the magical kingdom, just as you are. I just never learned how to use my abilities. I inherited my mother's broach, which I thought was the power, until recently." She said as she lowered her head.

"Maybe I can help you with that. I am a giver of gifts. I am limited in what I can do. Perhaps I can give you the gift of knowledge. A little training may set you in the right direction."

"Thank you, and after we are done, could you help us get to Lapland? There is a woman there we have to find."

Gerda turned her attention to the reindeer again, as the sleigh began to descend toward the ground. There below, hidden in the tree line, was a large complex of houses. As they landed just outside, Gerda turned and smiled at him. "You can't see any of this from above. It is camouflaged." Nicholas turned and smiled at her, as he laid a finger by his nose. She had learned another of his secrets.

Chapter Seven: The Secret Land Of Nicholas

Gerda stepped down, onto the frozen ground, as she looked around. Nicholas walked ahead and waved his hand as a dome appeared above them. The structure extended from one side of the complex, to the other, then enclosed the entire section of the mountain.

"It is a protection, that keeps those out who do not need to be here. To those on the outside, there is no clue that we exist. If they approach, they are transported to the other side, and they do not even know that they passed through."

"They cannot see or feel anything?" Gerda asked.

"Exactly! Mortals are best kept in the dark about magic. If not, there would be too much danger. If they knew, how many magical creatures walked among them, unseen or masked." Nicholas tried to give her as much information as she needed. He knew she was not ready to know everything just yet.

"So, what happens here?" She asked.

"This is my domain. Like the others have Spring, Winter, Fall, and Summer, I and a group of others have the magical days that we have power over. In this complex of hidden buildings, myself, the reindeer, and a group of rescued dwarves work to grant wishes in the form of gifts."

"I knew it, you visited me as a child. You left things for me over the years."

"Yes, until you went on a quest to save the one you loved. But even before that, you were distracted after your mother's death. I tried to distract you with my gifts. You did not deserve the pain that was inflicted on you. Freya should not have died so young. She was not destined to die at all. She had a long life ahead of her. When the Snow Queen took her life, she was not entitled to do so. She should pay for this deed." Nicholas' voice sounded cold for a moment.

"Why didn't the magical Kingdom do something about it?"

"It was believed that the Snow Queen was sided with the devil himself. We knew we had no power over him. We later learned he had abandoned her. Since, her punishment was decided, she is to be stripped of her power."

"Why has it not been enacted?" Gerda could not hide her disgust for the queen.

"We had to choose a vessel, to enact the revenge. Then, we learned there was one, destined to enact the punishment for us." Nicholas watched what words he spoke.

"You were waiting for me, weren't you?"

"I have said too much. All I can add is, you were not ready to carry out your task until now.

The power you inherited is surfacing. You know, you are much stronger than you ever imagined. And stronger, you will become. You just have to embrace the great power of love, you have inside. It is the greatest power you could ever have. Love can melt any frozen winter."

Nicholas led Gerda into the large doors in the main building. Inside, the warmth of the huge fireplace wrapped them with the feeling of a comforting blanket. Gerda embraced the heat. It had been some time since she felt this good. The chill in her cheeks faded, as she found her way to a huge chair near the fire.

Nicholas left her for a time, and came back with a huge mug, filled with a sweet-smelling liquid. He smiled at her, as she took the drink in hand, and lifted it to her nose. She smiled as she knew what it was. The heat from the liquid coursed through her body and she truly felt thawed.

"Where do we go from here?" Gerda asked.

"For now, you rest. Tomorrow, we begin your training. If you are to finish this quest, you need to know how to hold your own against her. The power is already yours, the ability to use it is where I come in."

Gerda smiled, as she was pleased to know he would help her. She drank the hot drink, and settled back into the chair, wrapped in its warmth. It was not long before she fell into sleep. Nicholas sat across from her, and watched as she drifted off. He reached for her cup, and sat it down, as he leaned over and kissed her on the forehead.

"Gerda my love, I wish I could tell you all I know. But if I did, they would retaliate against me. I probably should not have even brought you here, but I have to give you a fighting chance. I promised your mother I would never let harm come to you. The Spring Witch took me by surprise. I will not let that happen again. You have the power to lead us all. You just don't know what you have inherited." Nicholas walked to the fire and lifted a poker to it.

"Tomorrow, I will set you on the right track, before I turn you loose on the greatest trial of your life. You will be ready. And if you are not, I will be watching, just in case. But for now, sleep well my godchild."

Chapter Eight: Of Magic And Memories

Gerda walked through Nicholas' compound. He seemed to live in an impenetrable fortress. Just past his welcoming room, Gerda walked down a hall to find a fortress of defensive weapons. She studied them one by one, wondering what purpose they would have with such a peaceful man.

"Impressive, aren't they," Nicholas spoke softly as he came up behind her.

"Yes…but you don't seem the type to have such things. What are you defending yourself against?" Gerda asked, trying not to offend her host.

"There is more here than you know. I have a responsibility as a Guardian. I, like the others in my league, are responsible for keeping a certain balance in the world. If one of us were to fall, then the others would take up the slack as possible. But if two of us were unable to do our duties, the balance would be lost. I would not want to see that day."

"How did you become a Guardian? Were you appointed?"

"No, we are in our own way, born into it. There is a supreme entity that chooses each of us for our position. We were watched and guided as we grew to adulthood and were deemed worthy. It is not for everyone. That is why there are so few of us, and our appointments, last for hundreds of years." Nicholas said turning to smile at her.

"Hundreds of years? How old are you?"

He laughed as he opened his mouth. "On my next birthday, I will be 192 years old. I will have outlived everyone in my original family three times over."

"Do you not have anyone who can age with you?" She asked.

"If you mean in the human realm. No, everyone I knew and will know, will not last my lifetime. There are exceptions though. I have the other Guardians and some magical beings. The reindeer are almost as old as me. And then, I have met a few witches, wizards and such, that will be here for quite a long time."

"Witches live longer lives?" Gerda turned her attention to him.

"Yes, they do not die easily. They can live to be a couple hundred years old. As long as they do not renounce their magic."

"You mean like my mother did?" She said as her heart sank.

"Yes Gerda, like your mother. You see, she gave her magic up to marry your father. It shocked even me. She was stronger than any witch I had met. Even stronger than the Snow Queen. When she turned her back on the magical world, she became for the most part a mortal, with little power. She placed the majority of her strength and abilities in a broach, in case she needed it. She was not stupid. She knew there was a chance her sister would go insane. She kept it as a backup plan."

'Why would she do this?" Gerda spoke with a pained sound in her voice.

"Because she loved your father, and she wanted a life for herself with him. Then Kristoff came soon after, and then you. She loved you all more than you could ever understand. So much so, that she died to protect you from the queen." Nicholas' voice trailed off.

"You saw how she died?"

"Yes, all of the magic realms know how she offered her life to protect us all. I watched over her you know. I knew what she was about to do, but I could not stop her. She was allowed free will, and I thought she would win this battle, with her other sisters behind her. If it was not for that damn mirror, she would have beaten the queen."

"I have the broach. It was given to me after her death, as well as this cloak. I keep them close to me."

Nicholas walked closer, and touched the broach, as Gerda extended it to him. He smiled as a tear ran down his cheek. He tried to hold back his emotions but he was weakened by the sight of it.

"I made this so many years ago. It was a gift to her as a young girl. I blessed it with magic and instructed her on its use. She did so love flowers, that is why I fashioned it to look like this."

"I knew it was magical, every time I touched it, it would glow and become warm," Gerda whispered.

"Has she come to you?"

"Who, my mother?" She asked.

"Yes, if you possessed this, then she would have the ability to speak to you."

"Yes, when Kai disappeared, I was distraught and she appeared to me. I thought at first, I was imagining things. Then I knew it was too real."

"Have you shown signs of inherited power?" He asked.

"Yes, but only just recently. Why?"

"Because you are linked to her, through the broach. She is bringing forth your power. She knew you were destined. She wanted you to be ready for the fight before you."

Chapter Nine: Souls Connecting

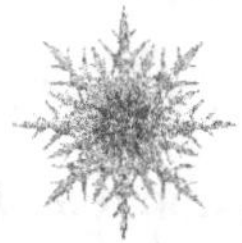

Nicholas led Gerda through the halls, until they entered a large work area. Gerda lit up as she spun around on her heels. The room was filled with every sort of gift imaginable. She took a deep breath, as she let out a giggle.

"You made these?" She said taking his arm in hers.

"Yes, with a little help. It is part of my role as a Guardian. They help keep balance in the world."

"This is so wonderful."

"It is where I crafted the broach, among so many other things over the decades. It is also why I have the armory. There are dark forces in the world that would just as soon see me gone."

"With the protections, you can spread your gifts around safely." Gerda smiled as she finally knew what he was all about. "If my mother was still residing in the broach, can I call on her?" Gerda asked.

"Supposedly. The power she placed here, held her essence and so much more. In time, it will diminish. As with anything in life, it has a timespan. As your powers grow, you will not depend on it so much. So, it will not drain as fast, but if you take on the Snow Queen, you will drain it I fear."

"So, what you are saying is, if I use the power to save my friend, then I will lose what is left of my mother?"

"Yes, my dear, I am afraid that is how it works. But bear in mind, she has already been dead for quite a long time. It is beyond anyone's power to bring her back. I couldn't even if I tried."

Gerda turned away and held tight to the broach. Somewhere deep inside she had always hoped she would find a way to bring her mother back. Then she realized those were just childhood dreams, and she was not a child anymore. She might not have lived almost a decade of her life, but life did not wait for her. As an adult, she had to let go.

As the night wore on, Gerda wore down. She was tired, there had been too much traveling and fighting. She needed rest. Nicholas led her to a special room he had set up for her. It was warm with a roaring fire and a big bed in the corner.

As she sat down, she felt the softness of the feather bed wrap around her body. She had never known such comfort. She wondered how life was for Kai. He surely did not have such comforts in the presence of the Snow Queen.

As Gerda drifted to sleep, she held tight to the broach. As she wrapped both her hands around it, a light began to glow from within. She held tight as she drifted off to sleep, and began to speak. "Kai, I wish I could know you are ok. If only I could talk to you." Her words drifted off as she entered a dream world created by the broach.

Gerda felt the shaking feeling, as her mental state was awakened to the dream world. She sat up and looked around. She did not know this place. It was cold and hard as ice. She looked down at the floors and realized it was frozen. This was an ice castle.

She looked around and saw the great hall. There was no one there, at least no one she could see in the darkened state of the place. She walked forward, and moved along near the wall, so no one could come at her from behind.

In the distance, she saw the great mirror. She studied it, not knowing what to think of such a thing. The glass was broken. The whole thing had been shattered, and someone for some reason, had been putting the pieces back in again. Why would someone want to do that, she thought to herself.

She reached out to touch the mirror, just as someone called out to her. "Stop, you don't know what you are doing. It has taken me half my lifetime to rebuild it. If you shatter it, I will have to do it all over again." The man's voice called out from the darkness.

As he moved forward, the light from the moon outside lit his face. Gerda went to him and raised a hand, tracing the outline of his features. She smiled as she recognized his face. A decade later he was still so handsome.

"Kai, it's you, isn't it?" Gerda choked on her words.

"Gerda, you are all grown up now. How are you here? How is this possible?"

"It's not possible, I am not here. It is magic and maybe even a dream. I will be with you soon. I promise, I am on my way to you now. It has taken me so long to find you, but I will come to your rescue. Even if it takes the last bit of power in my body, I will free you from this witch."

"I do believe you. Trust me, that is a lot, being I have not believed in anything in years. I have missed you so much. She tried to take you from my mind, but I have fought back."

"Stay strong, I am not far away. I have had help to get this far. Just believe me, I am ready for the fight." Gerda breathed deeply as she wrapped her arms around him.

Kai held tight to her, even in the dream state, he could feel her next to him. A light within him, that had dimmed to almost nonexistence, began to grow. He had hope again. A smile crossed his face in the dream, and in the physical world where his body lay on a frozen slab.

From the corner of the room, the Snow Queen approached. She studied the boy, and wondered what manner of state he was in. His lips moved as he lay there. His body jerked and moved about. The queen listened as his lips formed words. "Gerda, please don't go. Please don't." Then he fell limp as if the spell had left him.

The queen stood staring. She knew he had no power to bring such magic to life. She looked in the mirror. Had he pulled some enchantment from it? How could he? A mortal would never be able to wield such power. This came from outside the castle. A sinister look came from her eyes. If someone was invading her territory, she would be ready for them. No one crossed the Snow Queen and lived.

Chapter Ten: Freya

Gerda awoke early. She had slept hard. Her connection with Kai had drained her. She was not an experienced witch. She was a novice, a beginner. Still, she felt some comfort from the exhaustion. She had been reunited with Kai, or at least, the man he had become.

Gerda sat up in the feather bed smiling. She had lost her happiness somewhere along the way. The pain and struggle had finally paid off if only in a dream. She remembered her smile, it used to be a part of her every day. Then so much was taken from her.

The loss of her mother was more than any child should have had to deal with. Then, the loss of Kai as well. She knew deep inside, that he had not died, but still, it hurt her to lose him. All those years passed in the blink of an eye. They had both lost too much time apart. She thought in Kai's case, at least he got a chance to live those years. She had been robbed of them by the Spring Witch's magic and sleep spell.

Gerda turned and dropped her legs off the side of the bed. The floor was cold, but then what else would it be, in a winter-filled mountain? The fire in her room had burned down low. It made no difference, being she was getting dressed.

As she pulled on her clothes, she held tight to the broach for a second. It warmed her hands, and then radiated over her whole body. She smiled as she felt the magic envelop her. It felt like a warm hug from her mother. Gerda needed that, after all she had been through.

Without thinking, Gerda opened her mouth and spoke out loud. "Thank you, Mother. I needed that."

And just then a voice spoke back to her. "As did I, my love."

Gerda turned to look around the room. She was not alone. She shook her head. She was awake. This was no dream. The voice was one she knew. She held tight to the broach, as she opened her mouth to say one word. "Mother."

Nicholas was walking down the hall when he heard the voices. He stopped and listened in for a second. He was sure there were two distinct voices. He feared for Gerda's safety. He wondered if the Snow Queen had made her way through his defenses. That, he would not allow.

As Nicholas threw open the door, Gerda jumped back in fear of what was happening. She saw the uneasiness in his face, as he came towards her. He scanned the room to find the invader that had gotten past the fortress. There was no one.

"I am so sorry Gerda. I heard voices. I thought someone had come for you. I did not mean to invade your privacy." Nicholas looked down to the floor, ashamed of his actions.

"No. You were right. There were voices in here. Mine and another." Gerda tried to explain.

"Who? Did someone try to harm you?"

"No. I don't know how to explain. I just spoke, and heard a reply. Gerda was scared he would think she was insane.

"Then, who was it?" Nicholas said excitedly.

"It was me." The voice returned.

Nicholas looked around but saw no one. "Whoever you are, show yourself. I am not finding this amusing anymore."

As Nicholas commanded, the sound of the voice continued, as a light formed in the room. Swirling around in a sweeping motion, the light grew in form and started to show a dark figure from within. As the light pulled inside the form, it took the shape of a woman.

Nicholas moved to Gerda's side and took her hand. She was shaking, as her fear took her over. She had gone from a state of happiness to terror in minutes. The figure's darkness faded, as the features of the woman came into view. Her long blond hair fell over her shoulders. She stood there in innocence, as Nicolas handed her a blanket to wrap around her naked body.

As he looked at her, he knew her face. Nicholas swallowed hard as he called out her name. "Freya."

"Nicholas. I had never hoped to set eyes on you again."

"Freya, how could this be? You died. How are you here with us?"

"My magic is still alive within the broach. I guess my daughter is quite the witch, to use it to bring my spirit back from the afterlife." Freya spoke as she looked at the woman before her. "Gerda, is it you? When I left, you were a child. Now, look at you."

"Mother, I don't understand. I encountered your magic before, but you are different."

"It is this place. Nicholas embedded so much magical energy here, that I can draw on it to take form again. That, and the power in the broach, have allowed me to come here. I feel recharged."

"And, as long as you reside here in these halls, you will be alive again."

Chapter Eleven: Of Training And Gifts

As Freya dressed in clothing Nicholas had stored away, he led Gerda down the hall into the living room. He placed his hands on Gerda's shoulders, and tried to think of the words to advise her, on what had just happened. This was such a confusing situation, and he was worried.

"Gerda. I know what you saw back there. It is much to understand, and I am sure you are confused by it all."

"No, not really. You have to remember what I have been through. I mean, my mother died at the hands of her sister, who just happens to be the Snow Queen. That same magical creature, abducted the boy I loved, and has held him captive most of his life. Then, I go after him, one of the other sisters captures me, and puts me to sleep for almost ten years. I end up escaping, then find an enchanted reindeer, and come face to face with that same woman who did much of this. Now I have to battle her for Kai's soul. Oh, and did I mention, my mother is back from the grave, in the form of magic? And then, there is you, who defies explanation."

"Yes, I would say that just about sums it up," Nicholas said laughing.

"I know she is not the woman she was. That woman died. My mother is no longer a flesh and blood person. Still, this person in the other room is essentially my mother." Gerda put her hand to her head, which had begun to hurt. "So, can we say, she is still my mother?"

"Yes, by all rights, she is Freya. I felt her consciousness as she took form." Nicholas tried to hold back his concerns. "She is as much your mother, as if she was standing here in human form.

But, as I said before, this place is allowing her to be, for lack of a better word, alive. She will never be able to leave this fortress. If she does, her power will begin to fade. She will then cease to exist completely."

"Then, I guess that says it all, huh? I should learn to like this grand complex you created." Freya knew she had to be grateful, for the chance to regain her life. Still, inside she was angry at the idea she had no chances outside this realm.

"Regardless of the situation, Freya we have your back," Nicholas interjected.

"Yes, but I have a concern. I have been learning to use the power that I inherited from you. How does this affect me? I need that power to rescue Kai from the Snow Queen." Gerda turned from her mother to Nicholas, looking for an answer.

"You don't need anything from the broach. You had this power inside you all along. You were a blessed child. Didn't you ever notice that you were always protected from harm? You have a gift of enchantment all your own. Your mother's power, only coaxed you to tap into your abilities."

"Then, I can take on the queen on my own."

"No, you most certainly cannot. My sister is insane, and a person with too much power. You could die."

"You mean like you did?" Gerda jabbed back at her.

"I thought that with my sister's help, we could defeat her. It was that damn mirror, she pulled so much power from it. It was easy for her to take on anyone, magical or not."

"Well, she doesn't have the power of the mirror anymore. It was shattered." Nicholas added.

"What happened to the pieces? If she gets them back, she can reassemble it." Freya became edgy.

"She took Kai to her castle, over the years she has reclaimed most of the pieces, and has forced him to reassemble the mirror," Gerda said as she turned to look at her mother. "But she will never finish it. There is a piece of the mirror that is missing. If I have anything to say about it, she will never get it."

"Where is this piece she cannot locate?" Freya asked.

"It resides within Kai's heart. It came to him the day we moved from the mountain to the city. The piece of glass floated downwards and lodged in his eye. It then made its way deep inside, darkening him."

"Is she aware he has the shard?" Nicholas hoped she did not know.

"She has no idea. If she did, she would have ripped it from Kai's body already." Freya spoke over him.

"Then we have a chance. Gerda, you need training if you are to stand up to such a powerful witch." Nicholas spoke as he led her down the hall to the last door there.

As Nicholas opened the door, inside was an armory and training room. The space was huge, almost larger than should have been allowed in his house. Gerda studied the auditorium-sized room. She smiled as she looked around. She knew there was magic at hand.

"This in no way could be inside the building I entered," Gerda said laughing at him.

"Yes, my dear, this is a magically created space, that is hidden in the smaller realm you just walked out of." Nicholas looked around at his handywork. He was proud of himself. "There will be time for learning of these sorts of things later. Now, it is time for you to train. You have the power, and I will show you how to use it.

"With your permission, I would like to help. I mean, after all, she inherited this from me. Who better to show her how to take on such a creature? Without the mirror, and with proper training, you will be able to do what I could not." Freya moved to the center of the room and extended her hands to both of them.

"Welcome home my dear one," Nicholas said with a smile.

"It is good to be home again. Now let's get to work."

Chapter Twelve: The Frozen Heart

Kai was rattled from his sleep. He felt the chill in his bones. The room was so much colder and darker than usual. As he opened his eyes, he felt the sting of the frost that coated his lids. He was terrified of what was happening without even looking around.

As he tried to sit up, he pulled at his right arm, but it would not move. Then he tried the other, with the same effect. As he moved to sit up, he knew his body was too cold, as his vision went out of focus, and his head felt like it was spinning.

"Funny, what the cold can do." The voice came from the other side of the room. "I can build the most beautiful structures you could ever imagine. I can make intricate snowflakes that stagger the imagination. And if I want, I can kill those who oppose me with a simple flick of my wrist."

"Why are you doing this? I have always cooperated with you. I even rebuilt that hideous mirror of yours." Kai was tired of fearing his captor.

"That is interesting." She said moving in closer. "You are very brave now. You never were before. You were like my tame puppy." She laughed. "A lap dog at my command. So, what has changed?"

"I don't know what you are talking about. I am still here…still your captive." Kai felt the hardening of his lungs and throat, as he took in the frigid air, she surrounded him with.

"Silly boy, you were talking in your sleep. I heard you call her name. I know Gerda is near, but it will do you no good. By the time she gets here, you would be dead. Just another frozen statue in a long line of those who displeased me."

"Yeah, no one survives you…except the bear." Kai's words spit back at her.

"Stupid boy, you know nothing of the bear." The Snow Queen's voice betrayed her, as it showed how much he had gotten under her skin.

"I know who and what he was. He was King Valeman of the Summerland."

"How do you know that?" She screamed. "He would never tell you of his shame."

"The real shame is you. He has no shame, he is merely a man remade into a bear, for your amusement. Is that why your heart is so frozen? After all these years you couldn't force him to love you." Kai ripped into her with his words.

"I should just go ahead and kill you right now. It would be no great loss."

"Yes, but it would. You see, without me, your mirror will never be completed." Kai did little to hold back his anger. "The bear cannot do it with his claws. Any you…. you can't do it yourself. It dawned on me long ago, that if you could have reconstructed the mirror, you probably would have. For some reason, you can't touch it, in the state it is in."

The Snow Queen raged as she paced back and forth. Her breath flew outwards so quickly, that a mist of ice and snow flew out all around her. Then she stopped and turned towards him. She raised a hand, and shot a blast of cold wind and ice in his direction.

"Enough. I will kill you now and be done with it."

"No!" A growling voice came from the doorway. "You will not harm him any more than you have."

The queen spun around to see the great white polar bear standing on his hind legs. She lowered her hand and the assault on Kai ended. Cocking her head to one side, she smiled at the bear. She had not heard him defy her in some time. She was amused by this.

"My my, someone found his backbone. How long has it been?" She said laughing.

"Long enough, for me to have known better, than to allow you to do this." Valeman's voice came from under the growl.

The Snow Queen stopped in her tracks. It had been so long since she heard his real voice. It triggered her memory, and the image of the man that was, came to her. She smiled for a moment, as she realized the man she wanted, was still in there somewhere.

"And what is to say, I will not just kill you both, and be done with it all?"

"It wouldn't be to your advantage. Kai is right, you need him, or no mirror. And as for me, I have done so many more dirty jobs for you, than I ever want to remember. You would find existing without me to be problematic."

"The mirror is nearly done. I could still finish it." Her expression changed to one of insanity, as she looked around at the black walls of the room. She, for a moment, had no grasp on reality.

"It is true, you might find a way to finish the work. If you had all the pieces." Kai called out.

Then the Snow Queen's expression changed to one of anger as her eyes glared at him. "What do you mean by that?"

"I know how many pieces you have that need to be put in place. There is one missing from the pile." Kai said smiling at her.

"You are lying!" She screamed at him.

"No, he is not. He is right, there is a piece you do not have, and will not have access to if you harm him." The bear growled at her.

"So, you have both turned against me." The queen floated in and out of mental imbalance. "You will both pay for this. Maybe, I will start by locating your friend Gerda. I know she is trying to come for you. The obstacles I have put in place, have failed to stop her. Maybe, I just need to show you all, what it means to cross me."

The queen spun around in the middle of the room, shooting snow and ice in all directions before disappearing completely. Kai screamed out, as she faded from the room, but nothing could stop her.

Chapter Thirteen: We All Wear Disguises

"What do you think she will do?" Kai said as he sat shivering on the floor.

"She will go after the girl, but I think it will do her no good." The bear answered.

"Why do you think that?"

"Because I come and go from here, as I please. I travel the frozen lands surrounding this place. I even talk to those who I meet along the way." The bear laughed. "She has no idea, the number of friends I have made, outside these walls. And they tell me things."

"Really, what do you know bear?"

"Well, for starters, Gerda is closer than you think. Even the Snow Queen has no idea how close she is. The Guardian named Nicholas, has Gerda hidden in his fortress. He is training her to use her inherited power."

"Gerda has never had powers. She was simply mortal."

"Oh Kai, there is nothing simple about that girl. She was born of a witch and from a witch family. Gerda's mother came from a very powerful line. Do not underestimate her abilities."

"Will she be able to defend herself against the queen?" Kai asked timidly

"Gerda just might be more powerful than the whole witch clan." The bear explained as he ripped at the restraints, holding Kai to the floor. "She has made contact with you I assume."

"Yes, last night she came to me in a dream state. I wasn't sure if it was her at first. She is different now. The time apart has changed us both, I guess." Kai said, flinching, as the bear removed the shackles from his wrist. "Thank you."

"I couldn't let you stay here like this."

"I do thank you for that, but also for defending my life. In her insanity, I think she would have killed me, in spite of her need for me."

"That much is true. It would be worse if she knew what resided inside your chest." The bear said as he turned to walk away.

"Thank you for that as well. I know it is not your secret to deal with, but I owe you more than I can repay"

"For now, let us not count the score. We have work to do, before she comes back."

Kai and the bear headed to the large hall that housed the mirror. On another part of the mountain, the queen floated in the air, as the winds of winter swirled around her. She looked downwards, to the compound that Nicholas had constructed, to keep those like her out.

"You are powerful Nicholas, but I will have my revenge. No matter how many magical charms surround you, there has to be a flaw somewhere."

The Snow Queen spoke as she studied the shield that surrounded the grounds.

As Nicholas continued his training with Gerda, Freya stood near the front window. She felt uneasy. Something near was making her nervous. She scanned the surrounding areas until she found what she already knew. She saw her sister.

Freya didn't disturb Gerda's training; she knew could she go to the edge of the compound safely. Freya had to confront the one who killed her, and was trying to harm her family. As she watched the queen's movement, she headed out the front door and to the edge of the protective shield.

Freya walked across the land, looking as normal as the last day she was alive. To anyone who saw her, they would not have known she had been killed, but Freya knew it. As she walked, she remembered her death, and being ripped from her family, that made her angry.

"You have nerve coming here!" Freya called out from behind the queen.

As her words traveled through the air, they reached their mark and the Snow Queen's face changed. For a single moment, her frost-bitten heart raced with warmth, and the memory of one she loved. She turned slowly, daring not to hope the impossible could be true.

"Freya, is it you?" She questioned.

"Yes, I am here. Returned from a place of limbo." Freya's words were cruel and cold.

"I did not mean for it to end the way it did."

"You mean. when you killed me"

"It was the power of the mirror. I could not control it." The Snow Queen insisted.

"Oh Elaida, it is no different from when you killed our parents." Freya used the one thing she knew would rip at the queen's heart. "You destroyed our family, and spread us in all different directions. Did you believe I could forgive that? Then of all things, you killed me, separating me from my children and husband, for all these years. Just because of your thirst for power and control.

Your day is coming, and my daughter will deliver your destruction. I only hope I can see your downfall, as she destroys everything you created."

Freya turned to go back to the complex as the Snow Queen began to drift downward. She tried to find words to say to her sister. Anything that might have helped, but there was nothing more she could say. She knew it was all true. In her insanity, she had killed so many. It was true it all started with their parents. She feared where it would all end.

Chapter Fourteen: Gerda To Infinite Power

"Gerda, you cannot hold back. When I attack, you have to fight back with all you have." Nicholas said angrily as he shook his head.

"I'm trying, but if I do the wrong thing, I could hurt you," Gerda screamed.

"Do you think she would hold back? Do you think she worries about you being OK?"

"No, she does not. She is ruthless and has no regard for anyone." Freya interrupted as she walked through the door.

"Mother, I don't know how to fight like that. She practices dark magic."

"Yes, she does, and she will kill you with it. If she has no use for you, she will dispose of you."

Freya became frustrated. "Do I need to remind you, that she killed me, her own sister? She killed our parents, all because they sent a boy away, that she liked. She has no limits to her evil."

"I didn't know about your parents." Gerda tried to wrap her mind around it.

"I kept it from you, along with so many other bad things a child should never know. But now, you have to focus. I do not want to lose another family member to this insane witch."

As Freya finished speaking, she turned away from Gerda and raised her hand in the air. As she spun around, she unleashed a blast of energy in Gerda's direction. The room lit up as the energy flew forward. Gerda's mouth fell open, as she screamed and threw a shield around herself.

The shield deflected the power blast, as she felt the energy within her rise to a place she had never known. Before Gerda could think, Nicholas and Freya attacked at the same time. This time, there was no playing as Gerda fought back. The knowledge of what the queen had done, made her stronger. She did not want to be the next victim. She had to be strong, not only for herself but also to save Kai.

The room filled with blinding light, as Gerda continued to raise her power level. Then in an explosive blast, she sent both Nicholas and Freya flying backwards. Her point had been made. It was anger that fueled her abilities.

"What the hell was that?" Nicholas said as he tried to push himself up from the floor.

"I'd say my girl just proved herself worthy. I think Elaida has something to worry about."

"Are you two OK?" Gerda said as she landed back on the floor.

"Yes, my dear, I think we are. That was impressive." Nicholas said as he moved towards and hugged her.

"So, you think I am ready for her?"

"I think you are ready for an army?" Freya said laughing.

Just as they stopped talking, the perimeter alarms went off. Nicholas looked quickly as he turned and ran for the door. He investigated to see if anyone had broken through the shield, but no one was there.

Freya came from behind. "Do you see anyone?"

"No. My alarms never malfunction."

"So, if someone was there, then the alarms would sound?" She asked.

"Would that do it?" Freya said as she pointed towards the huge polar bear heading towards them.

"Get ready ladies, I don't think this is going to be peaceful."

"Who are you, and why have you come here?" Freya called out.

"I come here in peace. I mean no harm." The bear called back from the edge of the shield.

"Wait, I think I know this bear. I saw him many years ago. He brought your things back to us when you died."

"Yes, it was I."

"Then you are the bear with the Snow Queen," Nicholas said angrily.

"Yes, with her, but not by choice. She put an enchantment on me. I was once the king of Summerland. I refused her hand in marriage and she cursed me. At first, I was a man by night and a bear by day. Then she made it permanent after she killed the one I loved. I have been trapped like this for so many years. I swear to you, I am in no way on her side. But I do know of Kai, and I will help you to rescue him in any way I can."

Nicholas turned his back to the bear and looked at Gerda. She shook her head yes, as he created an opening in the shield.

Chapter Fifteen: Alliance

The bear came through the opening as Gerda watched closely. She was ready for anything. After all she had seen, she did not trust in those she did not know. Still, she wanted to believe in this bear from her past.

Just inside, the bear came to Gerda and sniffed at her. Gerda looked at him, confused by his actions. She stared at him, looking deeply into his eyes. Something was not right; she was sure this was not his true form. He had not lied to her.

"Why do you look at me that way?" The bear asked.

"You came to my home when I was a child," Gerda answered him. "You brought back my mother's cloak and broach. I saw you from the window as you left them. I see in your eyes, the man you once were." And with a wave of her hand, the bear stood on his hind legs as he reclaimed human form.

"How did you do that?" he asked in amazement.

"It is just temporary. I cannot undo what she did, but I can alter it." Gerda explained.

"For this much, I am grateful."

Valeman turned from Gerda to Freya, and he stared. He knew this woman. She had come to the castle to stop the queen. She was a force of good, until the queen killed her. He was saddened to be reminded of her death. He was there that day. He had the sad duty of removing her body from the castle. He felt his heart break as he recalled that sad day.

The voices of the past echoed through his head.

"I warned you if you ever tried to take the mirror, I would turn loose all the demons from hell. Maybe I don't need them, I might enjoy doing this myself." Damian's laughter filled the room as he prepared to strike.

"No!" Freya yelled at him. "You will not kill her. We came with the intention of removing the mirror from her and taking her power. We do not want her dead."

"Ladies, I appreciate your cause, and I agree she should be punished. But this is my battle, not yours. The mirror is mine, I will have it and her life as well." Damian turned back to the Snow Queen. "Prepare to die."

As Damian unleashed his power, Freya turned to her sisters. "We have to save her. We do not have to like her to be family. Help me."

The sisters each raised their power, and once again Freya channeled it, but instead of Elaida, their source was now Damian. As she unleashed the power, Freya found her mark by hitting Damian in his back.

He flew forward as the power engulfed him. Falling to the floor Damian had only one recourse, he turned to Freya and blasted her with the full force of his power. As Freya fell to the floor, her hand let go of her sister.

Ragnhild fell to the floor and wrapped her arms around Freya. The other sisters looked on in disbelief. They never anticipated anyone would die. The Snow Queen herself looked on in disbelief, as her sister lay there on the floor.

She regained herself, once again pulled on her power as she had before, and took aim at Damian. As the sisters took her cue, they used the power of the three remaining sisters to attack him. Damian struggled as he regained his strength, and then drew from the mirror what he needed.

"Women I do not blame you for what has happened here today. This should have never been your fight. You were never meant to be here. For that reason, I will not kill you. You are to go back to where you came from. Each of you to your own realm, with no memory of this event ever happening." Damian breathed deeply, then with a wave of his hand sent the sisters flying through time and space to their own lands.

"Now you are mine." He regained his anger as he turned to find the Snow Queen gone. "Where the hell did you go? You know I will find you eventually." He screamed as he walked to the mirror. "And you…. you have caused quite a lot of trouble. Too much trouble to allow you to exist. If it was not her, it would be another coming to claim you.

Taking the mirror in both of his hands, he transported them both to the sky above the castle. Climbing higher into the sky he looked to the heavens. "I cannot destroy you, but there is a higher source that can."

As he transcended the clouds, the mirror began to vibrate. The higher it went the more it shook, until he reached the highest point, he had ever dared to fly. It was there the mirror cracked. A fine line of cracks ran the whole surface of the glass. As he flew around in a circle the glass shattered completely.

Flying on the winds in all directions, the glass went out to cover the earth below. There were large pieces and small ones. Some were small shards, while others were microscopic in size. As they landed, they were found by people from all walks of life. Some used the glass for windows, others found pieces the right size for eyeglasses, while others were the victims of the glass, when the small pieces pierced their eyes.

The result was the same, wherever and however the glass was found. The evil within changed the view of the receiver. If they looked through the glass, they saw the worst of the world. If the glass entered a person's body, it would eventually find its way to their heart. They would grow cold and hateful. No matter their true nature they were changed.

Elaida hid in the castle until she was sure Damian had gone. Things could not have gone worse for her. Without the mirror, she had reverted to a lower level of power. She felt the weakness from within her. It was like a drug was taken from her. One she had learned to depend on. She felt the withdrawal, and it made her want the mirror back no matter what she had to do to get it.

Making her way back to the staircase, she looked down to where Freya's body lay on the floor. The lower level was a mess of debris and rubble. Descending the staircase Elaida could not take her eyes off Freya. Something deep inside her was not right. She felt the pain of loss. Her cold heart did not allow this feeling. It was something she did not care for.

As she reached the bottom of the stairs, she fell to her knees next to Freya's lifeless body. She stared down with her icy gaze. Her hatred for her sister was gone. In a brief moment of humanity, emotions overtook her, she felt the pain of her parent's death, and then Freya.

Cradling Freya's body, she rocked back and forth. Holding tight, like she was cradling a child, Elaida screamed out in pain. "What have I done." She began to cry as she buried her face in Freya's shoulder.

"What the hell have you done?" A voice came from behind her.

Allowing Freya to slide from her arms, she turned toward the voice. "Things got a little out of control."

The big white bear looked around. It would seem that everyone was in a battle that day, he thought to himself. Walking over to Freya, he looked down.

"This is your handiwork?" The bear growled.

"It all went wrong. I lost control and my sisters attacked. And then Damian came." Her voice trailed off as she regained her composure. "My mirror, he took my mirror."

"It was never your mirror. It belonged to the Dark One and he took it." The bear jabbed at her.

"No, not taken. I cannot feel its power, he destroyed it." She began to shake.

Unseen by either of them, Damian walked in through the open doors. He observed the situation and how the Snow Queen was mentally destroyed. He began to laugh at how pathetic he found her.

"Oh Queeny, is this all that is left of you?"

Turning towards him, she saw the frame the mirror had once occupied. She screamed, as she stood and ran to the wooden shell. Running her fingers around the edge, she waited for the power to surge through her, but there was nothing.

"What did you do? Where is the mirror?" She demanded.

"I destroyed it. It was too much of a temptation for the likes of you." He teased her.

"The mirror could not be destroyed it was all powerful." She screamed.

The Snow Queen looked up as he walked away. Her brain raced with the idea that the pieces of the mirror still existed. She grabbed at the frame and took it back to the place it had sat before. A smile crossed her face as she realized what she had to do.

"The mirror isn't gone bear." She laughed as she ran to his side. "It is still there in pieces."

"Yes, pieces that have been scattered across the entire earth." The bear reminded her.

"Then we find them, one by one until the mirror is rebuilt." She said as she spun out of control.

Looking around she turned to the bear. "Clean up this mess, we have to get ready to work. Oh, and remove her." The Snow Queen said as she pointed to Freya.

The bear went about his work cleaning the mess and restoring the castle. And when he got to

Freya, he removed her flowing red cape, being careful to keep the broach attached. He looked at her sadly before he spoke. "I never thought you would die like this. If I hadn't been away saving my people, I might have been here to stop this. I will return these to your family, so they know what has happened. I wish you well on your journey."

Placing the items to the side, he took Freya's lifeless body outside and buried her near the beautiful ice flowers. Above from a balcony, Elaida watched. She stared as the bear placed her carefully into the ground. As she watched, she felt the coldness of her heart reharden. She turned to walk away as she continued to plan the return of the pieces of the mirror.

As the big white bear reentered the castle, he collected the cape and broach and headed towards the door. As he climbed down the mountain, he decided not to disturb the family. He left the items by the back door and knocked as he hid by the house.

Jorgen opened the door to find what had been left. Closing the door, he fell to his knees. He had tried to prepare for this outcome but it was one thing he would never be prepared for. The children came to his side, as he pulled them close. Freya was not coming home.

Chapter Sixteen: Kai's Last Stand

Kai paced nervously through the great hall. He had been alone there before, but now, so much more was on the line. His brain raced to so many places, none of them good. The microscopic piece of mirror located in his heart struggled against him to gain control again.

Passing by the mirror, he looked down at the nearly finished surface, he had spent much of his life working on. He looked down at his hands which had seen their fair share of cuts and damage, due to handling the sharp edges. It was not easy to hold back his disgust at his wasted years.

As he stared at the mirror, he thought about smashing it all over again. That would have solved nothing. He dared not risk the rage of the queen again, before the bear's return…or Gerda's attempt to rescue him.

As Kai stared at the mirror's surface, he saw the glow. He had never noticed it before. It was as if the mirror was living. He had never thought of it that way before. It was magical and based in pure evil. Then he felt the throbbing in his chest. It was the piece within him.

"You want it back, don't you?" Kai spoke feeling silly talking to an inanimate object.

The mirror flashed a brighter light aimed at him. It was not only alive but intelligent. Kai moved back a few steps, in fear of what was happening. He shook his head; he didn't know what to do. He feared the queen would emerge as this was happening.

"You can flash lights at me all you want; you will never get this piece back. I will die first."

As Kai turned, the hall began to grow colder. He knew what it meant; she had returned.

He shivered as she came closer. She had almost frozen him to death earlier. He dared not risk her rage again. Moving into the shadows, Kai watched as she glided into the room. A mist of snow and haze floated all around her.

Kai watched, trying to assess the situation. He could not tell if she was angry or not. Her expression seldom showed joy or happiness. She idled at hate and rage. Kai wanted to curl into a ball, and hide until the bear returned.

"I know you are hiding there in the shadows." The queen said nonchalantly moving past. "Come out, and let me see you in the light."

Kai came forward and stood in front of her. "Yes." That was all he said.

"No…You should say, yes, my queen. Show obedience boy."

"I am no longer a boy. I am a man after all these years." Kai snapped.

"You are so stubborn. You have learned nothing." She snarled. "You know I have killed people for less than what you just did. Just ask the bear."

"I already know the bear's story. If I were him, I would have killed you in your sleep." Kai screamed.

Kai turned away, and as he did, he saw the mirror's light pulsing. It seemed as if the more they argued, the more the mirror lit up. It was feeding off them, and the fragment Kai carried in his chest.

He moved towards the mirror and reached out a hand to it. The mirror was warm to the touch. It was coming back to life. He turned to the queen who was still fuming, he could not let her know. But, how could he hide it?

The queen turned towards him and cast an icy expression. "What are you doing over there?" She screamed.

He thought for a second, he did not know what to do. He could not let her come closer and see the mirror's light. He stepped between the queen and the mirror, but the glow became brighter.

"What are you hiding from me?"

"Nothing, nothing at all." He yelled back, as he turned and threw his fist into the mirror.

As his hand made contact with the surface, the mirror lit with the brightest light yet. As he touched it, a power was released through his body. As it flowed through him, Kai turned towards the queen. He smiled a wickedly evil smile as he threw a hand in her direction.

In an effortless motion, he turned loose a stream of energy straight towards the queen. Her expression changed, as soon as she saw he controlled the mirror. As the force hit her, the Snow Queen flew backward and her body was slammed into her ice throne. She could do nothing but let out a scream, as she realized the mirror had regained power.

Chapter Seventeen: Frozen Dreams

As Kai moved towards the queen to admire his handy work, the mirror emitted a blinding glow throughout the hall. Kai pulled an arm to his eyes to shield them, as a blast of magical power shot skywards. As it climbed higher, a boom sounded throughout the surrounding areas, like an explosion of magic had gone off.

Back at the compound, the fallout rang through the area. The ground shook as if an earthquake had started. Valeman fell sideways, as Nicholas grabbed a hold of him. Gerda let out a scream, as a large shelf came loose from the wall, toppling in her direction.

As she spun to move out of the shelf's direction, she threw out her hands. She had no idea what she was doing, but the shelf began to move backward away from her. She took a deep breath and started to laugh, as she levitated the shelf back into its original location.

The ground stopped shaking as Freya turned to her daughter. "Good job my girl."

"I didn't know I was doing it. It just came naturally." Gerda said smiling.

"You are capable of so much. You do not have to think to use your gifts." Nicholas said looking around the place. "Doesn't look like any damage is done. What could have caused that?"

The door flew open, as Bae pushed his way in. "Are you all OK?"

"Yes Bae. Do you know what happened?" Gerda asked.

"I don't know for sure, but it came from the mountain. It has to have been the Snow Queen's doing." Bae speculated.

"No, this is not in her realm of power. This was full energy. I haven't felt anything like this since…" Valeman froze in his tracks.

"Why did you stop?" Gerda asked.

"I think I know," Freya said putting her hand on his shoulder. "It was the mirror. Wasn't it?"

"I thought the mirror was shattered. How could it have power?" Gerda became scared.

"Something has happened." Valeman turned to Nicolas. "Do you have a way to see inside the castle?"

"No, my reach cannot penetrate her domain."

"Mine can." Gerda moved her eyes up from her frozen stance. "I can use Kai, see what he sees. If I can get in his head, we can communicate."

"Do it, but be careful. We don't know how that power was unleashed." Valeman reached out to touch her arm in comfort, but got more than he bargained for.

As Gerda made contact with Kai, the energy flowed through his body. She saw the queen collapsed over her throne. Then she saw the mirror's glow. She knew this could not be good.

"What did he do?" Valeman whispered.

"What are you doing here?" Gerda jerked back in shock.

"I was touching your arm when you initiated contact. I suppose I was dragged in with your magic." He tried to explain. "Don't be angry, we have worse things to deal with right now."

"Kai is channeling the mirror. We have to get him away from it."

Valeman studied the scene, as he thought of everything that they could do. "Can you get Kai to hear you?"

"I can try but he seems to be controlled by this. I don't think he could respond to me if he wanted to." Gerda said before calling out to Kai.

"Gerda, you can't be here. The mirror has regained its power. It will hurt you. The queen didn't even stand a chance."

"We have to help you. Valeman is with me, just tell us how to help."

"Go, before it knows you are here." Kai groaned in pain. "Oh no, it's too late. It knows you are here."

"Is there any way to stop it?" Gerda pleaded.

"Gerda, forgive me." He said as he thrust her backwards, with a wave of energy.

"What happened?" Nicholas said lifting Gerda from the floor.

"It was Kai, he blasted us, to protect us from the mirror."

"What do we do now?" Valeman asked.

"Gerda, you have to go. You and Bae must find the Lapland Woman, as you were meant to, before I intercepted you. Maybe she will have a way to take back control of Kai. For now, Freya and I have to make sure the queen does not regain use of the mirror. Even if that means finding the devil himself."

Chapter Eighteen: The Lapland Woman

Gerda quickly gathered the things she needed and headed for the door. Stopping short, she turned to her mother with a look of sadness. Freya knew what was going through her brain.

"You are ready for this." Freya tried to reassure her.

"Mother, I am so scared. I felt better before the mirror came back." Gerda sighed. "What if she takes the mirror back? I can't stop that."

"You have no idea how powerful you are. Elaida is powerful, but she isn't as smart or determined as you. Trust me, you will succeed."

"I want to believe, but she killed you."

"Yes, but you are so much stronger than I was. Nicholas will be here to back you up." Freya said trying to smile through her concern. "Now go, there is no time for talk."

Gerda turned and headed out the door where Bae waited for her. She faked a smile for him as she walked to his side. The reindeer snorted, as the heat from his nostrils rose into the air. They began to walk towards the shield, as Gerda looked back to her mother.

"They think I have a chance of winning this battle." Gerda lowered her head. "I'm not sure they're right."

Bae moved closer and rubbed his head against her. "If it means anything, I believe in you."

"It means everything." She smiled. "Do you know which way we are headed?"

"Yes, Nicholas gave me directions. This might move faster if we took to the sky." He replied.

"Can you do that? What if I am too heavy?"

"You aren't. Reindeer are built for a lot more than that."

Gerda stood back and looked at him. She had no idea how to climb onto his back. "Just swing a leg over me and jump up." Bae made a sound that resembled laughing as she flew up into position.

Gerda grabbed onto the collar that surrounded his neck as Bae started to run forward. As he moved, his big hooves ripped into the ground and threw chunks of earth behind them. He moved hard and fast, as they flew towards the top of the mountain range. Gerda held tight as she saw the edge of the cliff coming fast.

"Uh Bae, should we be in the air by now."

"Have faith Gerda, this is not my first flight. When it is time, we will fly."

As the cliff edge came, Bae shot past it and they flew. Gerda felt her heart beat faster, as she realized they were no longer on the ground. She held tight as she took in the sights around them. A smile replaced the look of fear she had once had. Bae flew faster than she had ever thought possible.

"How can you move so fast?" Gerda leaned in to ask him.

"Enchantment is a wonderful thing. Nicholas needs us to travel quickly. Once a year he circles the earth as a Guardian. On this journey, there are eight of us pulling his sleigh." Bae was proud of his abilities. "Imagine how fast that would be. Many cannot even see us in flight. Stealth is a wonderful thing."

"I can imagine. How far do we have to travel to get to the Lapland Woman?"

"There, see the smoke rising from the flat land ahead."

Bae came in fast as he lowered them down to the surface. The sound of his hooves clapped loudly across the land. It resembled drums being beaten hard. If the woman was not aware of their approach, she would soon be. Bae slowed as he came to the door of her house.

The short fat woman emerged from her doorway. She studied the reindeer and the woman who rode him. She did not know what to make of it all. She looked at Gerda hard, and assessed she was not a threat.

She waved a hand as she turned to walk back inside. "Come, you are welcome here. Just make sure the reindeer does not make a mess."

"Excuse me!" Bae became offended.

"Oh great, he also speaks. That's all we need, an enchanted reindeer."

"Look, we did not come here to inconvenience or burden you." Gerda became frustrated at the woman's rudeness.

"Then say your piece. I have things to do." The Lapland Woman said shaking her head.

Bae began to explain the reason they were there. He told her of Kai and the Snow Queen. Then he asked if she knew of a way to help them.

The woman walked around talking to herself. Bae looked at Gerda in confusion. They did not know if any of the conversation was meant for them.

"Maybe she has lived alone too long," Gerda whispered in Bae's ear.

"I would agree." He replied.

"Yes, you are probably right." The woman stopped her conversation to respond.

"We are wasting our time here." Bae blurted out.

"No, you are not. You are just impatient. And you called me rude." The woman laughed. "Are you unwell girl?"

"I do feel a little weak and tired. I think the cold has gotten to me." Gerda realized the woman was right.

"Sit, I will feed you, then you rest, but not the reindeer. He is on his own." The woman grumbled. "Then, I will give directions to the Finland Woman. She might be able to help. I have no magic to fight the Snow Queen. That woman is crazy, I hope you can defeat her. Freya should have done it years ago. She was the only one brave enough to try."

"You know of Freya?" Gerda asked.

"Yes, everyone does. She was destined to rule, then she married a mortal, and lived a life she chose. She was a good one, she deserved happiness." The woman paused for a second. "She came back many years later to battle the queen, and brought her sisters with her. She lost the battle and her life."

"I know the story," Gerda said quietly.

"How do you know? You would have been a small child."

"She was my mother," Gerda spoke with a tear in her eye.

The old woman came to her side and hugged her. Gerda was shocked at her kindness. She didn't know how to respond. Then the woman put food on the table for her, and motioned for her to eat."

"I will draw a map for you, to find Finland Woman. I wish I could do more for Freya's daughter." The woman turned toward Bae and looked hard at him. "You will protect her, or I will change your belief of the damage an old woman can do." She stopped and handed him food.

Bae thanked her, as he realized the woman had many sides, he was not aware of.

Chapter Nineteen: The Finland Woman

Bae flew through the air, while Gerda held tight to him. She was becoming frustrated, feeling they were wasting their time traveling around hoping to find information. She knew deep inside there was a reason for all this, but at the same time, she just wanted to go to the Snow Queen and take Kai.

The winds of winter blew hard against, as they flew headfirst into them. Gerda tried to shield her eyes, but there was only so much she could do, with the blizzard that blasted at them. Then she thought, maybe she could do better.

Raising a hand, she extended her fingers in front of her and closed her eyes. A glow extended from her hand, and began to spread in all directions around them. Gerda smiled as she realized this was all becoming easy for her. Soon the light she created, acted as a barrier against the wind and snow.

"You never cease to amaze me," Bae called to her.

"Sometimes, I am amazed as well." She giggled. "Never hurts to practice.

"I will just be glad when all this is done. I don't like being on edge and constantly trying to go places. I want to go home and be with my family of reindeer."

"Soon Bae, Soon." Gerda tried to reassure him. "Is that the place up ahead?"

Gerda pointed to the right and Bae looked hard at the little house in the distance. He studied the landscape as he descended to the ground. He came in fast, and then slowed as they came closer. It has to be the house, there were no others for miles.

"Gerda, keep your guard up, I do not feel good about this place."

"Should we go?" She asked. "I do not want to put either of us at risk."

"No, we have to do this. Nicholas would not point us in the wrong direction." Bae was certain of his words.

"OK, then I guess we knock on the door and hope for the best," Gerda said as she raised a hand.

"You are the chosen one." The Finland Woman said as she pulled the door open quickly.

"I don't know…what that means." Gerda was shocked by her words.

"Nicholas sent you, did he?" The woman spoke oddly, almost as if she knew more than they said to her.

"Yes, Nicholas sent us, we need help in a situation regarding the Snow Queen." Gerda tried to explain.

"Yes, the Snow Queen has something you desire. No…not a something…a someone. The man, who was once a boy…now a slave to her. No... the mirror. It lives." The woman kept spouting information before they could give it.

"How are you doing that?" Bae asked the old woman.

"It is all around you." The woman replied.

"What is?" Gerda asked.

"Time, it flows around all of us, the past, the future…the present. Your time was interrupted, buy a witch."

"Yes, and so was Kai's. The Snow Queen took and enslaved him to rebuild her mirror."

"The mirror. It is alive again. The boy rebuilt it, save one piece. It is hidden from her. The mirror knows where it is. It sent its power through him. She was the recipient of the blast. For now, she is unconscious." The old woman laughed. "Won't last long though. She will make him suffer for using the mirror's power."

"He didn't use the power willingly; it was channeled through him." Gerda was sure of it.

"No matter, it will be a battle between the witch and the mirror, to claim the boy, and retrieve the shard. Death, he will face, before the piece is removed. If it could be removed." The old woman's expression changed. "You must see your fate before the battle. One life, will end that day."

"You mean one of us will die?" Gerda became frantic. "Who?"

"Not for me to say. You can see it for yourself, then or now."

"You mean you can help me look into the future?"

"Yes girl, and you have to be quick about it." The old woman turned and walked to her table. There she had been cleaning fish. As she scooped up a bit of the meat, she covered it with spices and herbs offering it to Gerda. She looked down in disgust at the uncooked fish. She shook her head, but she knew it had to happen.

As Gerda took a bite, she felt odd. Her mind began to drift. Bae leaned in behind her, to stop

Gerda from falling to the floor. She slid back out of her chair and downward. Her head spun as she felt herself leave her body.

Gerda watched as the ice castle took shape before her. Kai was standing there near the mirror. On the other side of the room was the Snow Queen. She was regaining consciousness. She flew into a rage as Kai stood strong before her.

The queen drew on all of her power as she aimed for Kai. Gerda cried out "No," as she watched the queen unleash her power. Kai turned his head as if he heard Gerda's scream. For a second, he was distracted, then he saw the force of the blast coming at him.

The mirror glowed brighter as it fed power to him. He raised his hands and prepared to defend himself, but he was too late. The queen overpowered him. As he called out Gerda's name, his lifeless body fell to the floor.

Gerda screamed out in pain, as she saw him fall. Her heart was breaking, with the fear he was dead. Back in the Finland Woman's house, she screamed out in pain. The woman looked at her, as Bae tried to nudge her with his nose.

"No, she must come back on her own." She insisted. "If you distract her, she may not find her way back."

Gerda tossed from side to side before opening her eyes. She wiped away the tears that ran down her cheeks. She sat up slowly, and looked at Bae and tried to speak.

"He's gone. She killed him." Gerda choked on her words. "He had the power of the mirror and she still killed him."

"Things are not always as we see. Fate is funny that way. What she has done, you may undo." The old woman insisted.

"Then it is not too late?" Gerda whispered.

"Love has its own power. It is strong. Sometimes transcends death. Just have to believe."

"We have to go to the castle. I will save him. I have to. I will not allow our story to end this way. I will find a way to bring him back from the land of the dead."

"Be careful, for once he travels too far and mingles with the dead too much, he will not be able to come back to the land of the living." The old woman turned, and went back to her fish as they left her doorway.

Chapter Twenty: The Story Of The Snow Queen, The Dead, And A Girl Named Gerda

Nicholas prepared his sleigh as Freya joined him by the stables. She walked over to the reindeer, and stroked the back of one as she approached. She was troubled and Nicholas knew it. She avoided his eyes, as she came to his side.

"I want to be a part of this." She said calmly. "I need to make sure Gerda survives."

Nicholas turned to her, and took hold of her arm. "I know the pain you are struggling with. She is your child, but now she is a woman, and can defend herself."

"I know that, but it changes nothing in my mind." She choked on her words.

"Freya, you can't go with us. The minute you step outside these grounds, you will cease to exist. You wouldn't even make it to the castle to help in any way." Nicholas pulled her into a hug, as he continued to speak. "Let us do what we can, to help. If there is any way to save her, I will. But, do not sacrifice yourself to accomplish nothing."

Freya held tight for a moment and then pulled back. She knew Nicholas was right. Valeman came to them, trying not to disturb the moment they were having. He just stood for a moment, before joining them. He could feel the pain Freya was trying to hide.

"Is everything OK?" Valeman asked.

"Yes, everything will be fine, in time," Nicholas answered back.

"What will happen when I go through the shield?"

"You will revert to the form you were. We can block the enchantment while you are here, but

out there, we cannot stop her power over you."
Nicholas wished there was another way.

"Then, I will go on foot. The sleigh is no place for a polar bear." Valeman said as he walked to the outer edge of the shield.

As he passed through, Valeman felt the morphing begin. He fell forward on all fours as his body elongated. As he lunged forward, his body finished its change into the familiar form of the bear he had been. He looked back, before running at top speed through the trees.

"I have to go." Nicholas sighed. "Just stay here and stay safe, and I will bring her back to you."

"I know." Was all she said, as Nicholas sat down on his seat, and called out to his team.

~~~~~

One by ground, the others by air, they converged on the top of the mountain. Bae landed hard, still kicking forward as he approached the
~~~~~

outer door of the ice castle. Gerda leaped off his back and landed on the steps. She looked around studying the grounds. The great hall was just inside, and so was Kai.

Gerda shook her head, she was angry. Her days of being quiet and holding back were over. She told Bae to stand back, as she raised a hand to knock on the door. When it flew inward, almost ripping off its hinges, Bae just stared at her.

Stepping inside, Gerda moved cautiously. She had no idea what might have been awaiting her inside. As she moved forward, the door flew shut again, stopping Bae from following. He stood there watching, not knowing if Gerda did it, or some other force from within.

The polar bear ran up behind Bae, just as Nicholas swept down near them. Nicholas looked concerned, that they were stopped outside, and Gerda was inside by herself. He took off his hat and wiped away the snow that gathered on his face.

"Stand back, I will try to get us inside." Nicholas slammed the door with force, but it did not move. It did not even budge.

"There is more at work here than just a door being forced shut," Bae observed. "There is energy surrounding the building. It was put here to stop us, but not Gerda."

"How. This makes no sense. The Snow Queen could care less. She would love the attention, while she battles Gerda." The polar bear growled.

"It's Kai and the mirror," Nicholas added.

"He's dead. Gerda saw it." Bae shouted above them.

"He may be dead, but his spirit is still linked to the mirror." Nicholas felt uneasy, he was concerned about how much the mirror controlled Kai.

Inside the castle, Gerda moved forward carefully, watching everything around her. She expected herself to be scared, but she wasn't. She was angry. Her main concern was Kai. In front of her, she saw the great hall. It was just as it appeared in her vision.

In the center of the room was a large table. It shimmered with ice and crystals. As Gerda came closer, she saw Kai lying in the center of it. He was a stranger to her, being older, she only had the image from her visions.

Moving closer, she touched his hand. Her heart broke as she realized he was cold. He was truly dead. She had come so far, to be faced with this. Moving closer, she looked down at his face, as the tears ran down her cheeks.

Gerda leaned over, as she placed her arms around him. Her pain overtook her for a second, as she held tight. "I have finally found you after all this time. So much has been taken from us. It should have never happened this way."

As Gerda raised up, a tear fell from her cheek and landed on Kai's face. She looked down, as she felt a change in him. Gerda pulled back for a second, as a glow came over his face. Kai's body shook for a moment, as he drew in a deep breath. He was emerging from the land of the dead.

Gerda swallowed hard as she watched. "How is this possible?" She whispered.

"You did this." The Snow Queen said as she entered the room. "The power of love is great. It is the strongest power on earth. You have no idea how strong you are. How could you be so innocent? So pure of heart."

"I guess, I am just not as jaded as you." Gerda moved between the queen and Kai.

"You will not have him. Not if I have anything to do with it." The Snow Queen said as she raised her arms.

Unseen to Gerda, Kai sat up, and felt the warmth returning to his body. At first, he felt like a living zombie. He had no feeling, no control of his body. Then he felt it all returning, as he turned to see the queen about to strike at Gerda.

"No!" He screamed as the ice shards began to form, and move towards Gerda.

The mirror glowed brightly as Kai returned to the world of the living. He felt it within him, as he jumped from the table and stood by Gerda's side. She turned to look at him, as she extended a hand in the direction of the ice.

Gerda felt the power build within her, as she blasted back towards the Snow Queen. Kai looked at her in amazement, at the gifts she had acquired, since he had known her. He took from her cue and added the power of the mirror to hers.

The queen raised her power, turning loose the force of a blizzard in the room. The snow and ice flew hard Kai and Gerda. Her force of winter, wrapped around the circle of power, that surrounded and shielded them.

"You came for me. Even in death, you stood by me." Kai struggled to speak.

"I will always come back to you," Gerda said smiling. "Some things are meant to be."

Kai felt a tide changing inside him, as his heart felt like it was racing. He felt the love he had always experienced with Gerda. It overpowered him. He could feel his blood heating inside.

As he reached up to wipe what he thought was a tear from his eye, he pulled back a finger covered in blood. There on the tip of his finger was a shard of glass. Kai knew what it was immediately.

Gerda looked over at the blood and the shard. He handed it to her. He was glad to have it out of his body, but the glass could not be allowed to go back to the mirror, or the queen.

Gerda turned her palm upwards and let the shard roll into the middle. With a simple movement, she blasted the piece into microscopic dust. It was done, the Snow Queen would never have the power again.

Without the piece of mirror within him, Kai felt the mirror's power leave him completely. His heart was warm again, he felt all the emotions he had been robbed of, rushing back in like a dam breaking. Gerda sensed his change, as she launched a final assault.

Gerda blasted as hard as she knew how at the queen. Then she looked over to the mirror which still glowed. With a flick of her arm, Gerda sent it flying upwards through the roof. Outside, Nicholas saw the blast, and took to the sky to retrieve the source of evil.

As he reached out for it, he placed the mirror into a protective bag that dampened its power. Storing it within the sleigh, he flew as fast as he could, away from the location. The Snow Queen could never know where it was taken.

The queen screamed, as she saw the mirror being taken. "What the hell have you done?"

"Created an even playing field," Gerda called out over the sound of the storm surrounding them.

Gerda was done, she had accomplished almost all she had come to do. The queen was her last goal. As she raised her hands, she heard someone behind her. She turned, to see a somewhat familiar face.

"Who are you?" She asked.

"I am Damian." He said smiling at her.

"You mean…that Damian?" Kai asked.

"Yes, but don't worry, I am not here to harm you. I am here to help you get rid of her, once and for all."

Damian exerted his force and joined it with Gerda's. Together, they overtook the queen, ripping at her, bit by bit, until she fell to the ground. As they watched, there was less Snow Queen and more Elaida before them.

As she lay there on the floor, Damian walked over and looked down at her helpless body. The Snow Queen was no more. Elaida sobbed, as she realized, she was human again. Her power was gone.

"I told you; I would make you pay."
Damian stood over her laughing. "Now it is time to finish the job."

"What do you mean?" Gerda said moving towards him. "She is beaten."

"She has to die; it is the only way to know the Snow Queen is truly gone."

"No!" Gerda demanded. "I know she has done so many horrible things. She even killed my mother, but letting her live with no power, is more of a punishment than just killing her."

Damian looked down at her, and then back to Gerda. He smiled for a moment, as he thought about her life from that point on. "You were wronged by her. If you think this is fair, then I will let you make the call. You know, you have become quite a strong woman."

"You knew me before?" Gerda asked.

"Yes, Freya raised you well. Use that power wisely." He turned and walked away. "I have things to do elsewhere. I bid you adieu."

As Damian departed, the protection around the castle dissolved. The Polar Bear King stepped forward, entering the hall followed by Bae. As he walked, the bear began to disappear. The enchantment over him, was the final piece to fade. He had regained his humanity permanently.

As he reached the queen, he leaned down to look at Elaida. He extended a hand, and lifted her to her feet. He shook his head, and looked at what was left of the woman, who had made his life hell. Still, he pitied her.

Nicholas returned to the grounds and looked at the destruction within. "I guess I missed the good fight."

"Maybe, but in the end, we won the war. Maybe it is time we went home. I want to see my mother. She will be glad Kai is OK." Gerda sounded relieved.

"I think you are right. Valeman, are you coming with us?" Nicholas asked.

"I am going to stay for a while and make sure she can handle all this. Then, I will join you." He answered.

Gerda walked out the doorway and looked over the mountain. It was different now. The snow was melting. Everything seemed a little less frozen. She wrapped her arm around Kai's, and pulled him tight as they walked. "Seems like we had so many people interfering with our lives. Now, it is on our terms." They walked into the sunlight, hand in hand.

The End!

**Included at the end of this book, are the first two
chapters of G.W. Mullins' Best-Selling title
Rise Of The Dark Lighter Book One –
Dark Awakening**

CONVERGENCE
BOOK ZERO

MASS DESTRUCTION

G.W. MULLINS

The Convergence Book Zero
Mass Destruction
Is Available in
Hardback (978-1-958221-09-9),
Paperback (978-1-958221-08-2)
and various eBook formats worldwide.

The Frozen Heart

"I know not with what weapons World War III will be fought, but World War IV will be fought with sticks and stones."

Albert Einstein

"If we don't end war, war will end us."

H. G. Wells

THE
CONVERGENCE
BEGINS

Chapter 0 - The End Is Now

"Why do you look so scared, Comrade Patrick?" The Russian cosmonaut asked, as he laughed studying the other man's reflection in the glass of his console.

"I'm not scared, so much as I don't know how to react to the experience of floating free in space. I mean, this is the real thing." He replied.

"You chose to accept the position of captain of this spaceship they are building. What do they call it now? Discovery?"

"Who knows what it is called this week. All I know is, they are putting me through every training that is known to man." Patrick said, shaking his head as he turned to look out of the space station's window.

"I would not worry if they chose you, then they must be sure of your abilities. Besides, you may end up being one of the few who survive. Tensions are great, war is imminent. If your ship gets off the ground, you and the people living on it may be the last people of Earth."

"Wow, thanks…that was not too much pressure to put on me."

"Calm yourself, the spacewalk will commence in 15 minutes. You had better get suited up."

"Pavel, can I ask you something?" Patrick said staring into the man's face.

"Yes, what would you like to know?"

"If World War 3 does break out, would we still be friends?"

The Russian began to laugh, "What makes you think we are friends now? I am only kidding. We have known each other for some time. I do not trust very many people. You, I trust with my life. We would probably be friends no matter what."

Patrick turned and floated down the corridor. His stomach turned at the thought of what was before him. He doubted himself, and the role he would lead in saving mankind. If the war did not kill humanity, the state of the environment was about to.

The environmental crisis that was spreading across the earth was unrepairable. The planet would be uninhabitable in less than five years. The governments knew it was coming for decades, yet they did nothing until it was too late. Now, instead of doing whatever they could to save lives, they were on the verge of nuclear war.

A group of scientists came together and formed the concept of the ship Discovery. It would serve as a record of human life, and a way to preserve a small group of humans. The ship would feature the latest in space pod living, and feature holographic technology, that would create a world that looked just as the earth did, for the regions the groups of people would be taken from. In a sense, they would never know they had been relocated to the ship. There could be no mass hysteria if the people were unaware, they even left their homes.

The real challenge was, to get Patrick trained and the ship completed before the first nuke was launched. The estimated departure was to come in two weeks. There was no time for error or unsureness of the new ship's captain. Patrick knew this, as he began to pull on his space suit. Breathing deeply, he was no amateur and he knew it. Lives depended on him.

As the door opened into deep space, Patrick stared out in awe. It was everything he had hoped it to be. His fears were behind him, as a smile crossed his face. He checked his readings one last time as he floated in the doorway.

"Well, are you going to float there all day, or are you going out?" Pavel teased him.

"I am going out. Oh, and Pavel, don't let anything happen while I am out there." Patrick joked.

"What could happen? There is nothing going on here except space. Maybe the settlement on the moon's surface might drift past as you are finally going out the door."

"I cannot believe we finally settled the moon," Patrick said looking towards the lights on the surface. "Man, that is beautiful."

As Patrick finished his last words, he floated outwards away from the station's doorway. He breathed deeply, as he moved around and saw the earth below him. He didn't know what to think, being so far away looking in. He finally found his strength and courage.

Patrick turned around and looked back to the moon. The structures were very clear to him from his distance. They looked like a small city, like you would find in some quiet corners of the earth. Except, there were no quiet corners anymore. The days of quiet were gone years ago. They went with the plague that came after Covid. Too many lives were lost, too many mistakes were made. No one knew of the side effects the cure would have.

As Patrick floated deep in his thoughts, a bright light shot in his direction. He struggled to see what was going on. "Pavel, what was that?" He waited, but there was nothing except silence. Then a second blast, and he knew what was happening.

As the moon rattled, and then debris shot into space, a huge chunk of rock flew at Patrick. He pulled at his harness feverishly, quickly moving out of the way. Then as his body drifted in space, he turned and saw the destruction. The moon was blasted in two, separated almost down the center. The lights on the surface came from nuclear explosions. He was sure of that. "Pavel, do you hear me?"

"Yes, Comrade, it was nuclear in nature. Word is spreading across all channels. There have been explosions back home as well. You are ordered to come back to the station. We are at war.

It has begun…the end of life as we know it is upon us."

Chapter 1 – Six Months Ago

"Hostilities are growing between the United States and Russia. While the United Nations is struggling to bring some resolution, several other countries have entered the hostilities, many of which are communist. The fear of war is looming."

The sound from the monitor speakers echoed throughout the former NASA space center. The massive workforce stopped in unison, as they looked towards the screens which lined the massive halls. In that moment, there was no other sound, but the news anchor's voice.

Many bowed their heads in silent prayer, for a solution to the inevitable event that was coming fast upon them. Others turned back to their work. They knew if they did not finish as scheduled, there would be no reason to build the massive metal structure, that rested between the buildings in front of them.

Patrick walked the hall, making his way to the command center. As he looked out of the window, at the puzzle pieces before him, he could see the ship taking shape. He shook his head, thinking this ship was like something out of an old space movie. If it worked, it would be spectacular.

The ship was broken into several pod cities, which sat side by side on the outer platform. All of which would be connected by a main central ship. The ship even had its agricultural pod, to constantly produce food and oxygen. Patrick smiled, as he realized he would captain this massive starship.

His joy turned, as Patrick faced the reality, that only a select group of people would be chosen to go into space. He found it cruel that the whole process of saving humankind would be cloaked in deceit. Those left behind would certainly die as the global ecosystem disintegrated, from pollution or radiation.

He felt a lump in his throat, as he faced the reality, that family and friends would not survive. Today, that would not be his greatest concern. Discovery had to be finished on time. So far, that seemed like an attainable goal.

"It's beautiful, isn't it?" A female voice came from behind him.

"Yes, it is. I just never thought it would come to this." He answered.

"I am Major Carter. I am supervising the pod's construction and testing all holographic installations in the cities within."

"Hello, I am Alexander Patrick. I am for lack of a better term, the captain."

"I am aware. Don't let it overwhelm you. This is a great honor to be chosen to head this ship. You are going to save a lot of lives."

"Yeah, and they won't even know it. They will go to bed one night, and then wake up the next morning, not even knowing they are on a spaceship transplanted into a holographic world, not of their choosing." Patrick grumbled.

"It is necessary. If word got out that we were selecting individuals to go on this ship, or even that the ship existed, we would be bombarded with people trying to force their way onboard. We can barely handle the size of the group we are taking. There just is no fair way to go about this." She sighed knowing she was never going to make herself believe it, let alone another person.

"Will we make the deadline?" He asked.

"Yes, I believe we will, as long as no one sets off a nuke. Seems like many countries have their fingers ready to push the launch buttons."

"Carter, you are very high up in the government. So, you would know…what are the chances of anyone surviving if multiple warheads are launched?"

"Life on earth as we know it, would be gone. There are safer locations and chances some people would find safety, but radiation would wash over the planet. Whatever would still exist, would be changed, and civilization would crumble. All major cities would soon be uninhabitable. Ever watch a zombie movie?"

Patrick turned back to the window and swallowed hard. He knew she was right. Then, he felt guilty, he was going to survive the possible holocaust, while millions died. He thought hard and then forced the unsettled feeling to the bottom of his stomach. He had to be strong. People would be depending on him.

He turned back and looked at Carter. "What about you?"

"What about me?" She asked

"What will happen to you?"

"I will be going with you. I have been granted passage on the ship. You will need someone to head engineering, and I am as qualified as anyone." She said smiling.

"Good, I am happy you will be safe."

"None of us will be safe, until this ship breaks free from the atmosphere, and gets out of attack range."

"You think they would shoot us down? That is crazy." He said in anger.

"No, that is real life, and in a war, you take down the one with the advantage. They don't want to see us succeed, while they stay behind to die. In a rational world, I would like to think everyone would like us to make it into space. Then…there is nothing ration about nuclear war."

"I guess, we work to make this happen. No matter how we have to do it."

"I hear they have a series of training sessions for you. Including a spacewalk. I can only imagine what that will be like."

Patrick looked upwards, staring into the sky. He had never been outside the Earth's atmosphere. He craved the experience, but still, he had an element of fear inside him. He wondered if it was all too much too soon.

Carter walked over and placed her hand on his shoulder. He turned to her and smiled. He knew she was trying to comfort him, but he had his demons to deal with. She smiled back at him as they both turned to the window and looked upwards. Their future was right in front of them.

Chapter 2 – The Ship of The Future

The morning news brought the world one step closer to the brink. North Korea, once again went against threats from the world and tested another nuclear warhead. The explosion came with a warning to the United States. Any interference would result in retaliation.

President Jones, stood his ground, as he defended the country and his pride. Even he knew, there was no winning in this war. We were doomed, no matter who fired first. He could only hope to hold out until Discovery was launched.

The weeks flew past, as Patrick saw his spacewalk approaching. The ship began to take shape, as the massive dome cities were attached to the main body. In the days after, Patrick walked the ship and took in all he would be captain of. He had grown up watching Star Trek, and he tried to think of this as his enterprise. It was a far cry from being that advanced, but it was so much more than he expected.

As he entered the first dome city, the hologram, automatically engaged. An electric grid formed all around him, and as he watched, the shapes of metal walls and glass windows disappeared. Where there were once smooth metallic shapes, there were now glowing lines that converged together taking form.

On the massive floor before him, the shapes of buildings and grassy fields emerged. Patrick stood back in awe of the holograms. He had never seen anything like it before. In a matter of seconds, a small country town was erected.

Patrick walked in the field of grass, that swayed in the breeze. He kneeled and ran his hand through the blades. It felt real. He knew in his mind it was a projected material, but to his sense of touch, it was still real.

He fell back onto the ground. Laughing out loud, he could not contain himself. It was all real to him, from the plants to the sound of birds in the trees. Even the feeling of the breeze caressed his cheek. He couldn't tell the difference.

Then, he thought of those who would be transplanted there. They would not know either. They would just think, they were home. It was still a lie, but they would know no difference. At least he thought, they would still be alive.

"I see you have come to know Carson Corners."

Patrick flipped around to see Carter heading his way. "Yes, this is so much more than I expected. It feels like I am on earth. I did not know things like this were possible."

"It wasn't, until very recently, and then we kept it a secret since it has so many military applications."

"Something so wonderful, that could be used for so many good things, has to be hidden from those who would abuse it." Patrick reached out and touched the grass, trying to understand why people were abused so much in the world.

"Welcome to the real world," Carter said walking away.

"Well, almost. The world we soon would have lived in."

"This one has its advantages. Like health care, and controlled weather. You can even summon help if you know what to ask for. Watch this…emergency care needed, medical."

As she finished speaking, directly in front of them, a distortion in the holographic field formed. The image of a man took shape, as a brilliant light swirled in place.

"I am Holo-tech Medical Assistant 1, please state your emergency." The figure stood before them, as the light he emitted flicked and fizzled.

"Hmm, that is strange, he is having trouble taking form. I'll have to look into that, it should not be happening. Still, it is new, and there is always some issue to fix." Carter said staring at the hologram.

"PPPPPlease state your emergency." The hologram asked.

"There is no emergency. This is only a test. One that is failing miserably. Disengage Medical Assistant. This will have to be looked into"

As Carter spoke, the hologram disappeared into the electrical grid. Patrick watched in disbelief of the technology, as everything returned to normal. The hologram system was intelligent and could add to itself at will.

"Carter, if the people living here are not supposed to know about the hologram, how are you going to use the medical assistant?"

"Easy, he will appear, as if in a hospital setting or as a doctor making a house call. He can change himself to fit any situation, just like the holographic grid can adapt to fit the need. We can add terrain, add buildings, or add roads and land as a person travels. In most cases the hologram moves, the person does not."

"This will take some getting used to. All I ever saw a hologram do was perform in concert." Patrick said knowing he was out of his ballpark.

"Oh, you saw those disgusting holographic pop stars? They were awful, I am glad they have been phased out. Still, if we didn't start there, we would not have gotten to this point. Now, imagine a complete town or city like this in each pod, fully functional, programmed to expand and create new things as needed."

"I would say that is a lot of room for error." He laughed.

"Unfortunately, and that is why we are testing and perfecting before Discovery gets off the ground. In space, there is nowhere to find out, we made a mistake."

"At least, you will be there to help fix what may go wrong."

"I would rather get it right before liftoff."

As the two walked forward, the land before them, extended and continued in any direction they chose to go. The hologram seemed to work in every way, except where creating people was concerned. That seemed like the least of their problems.

Thanks for choosing this book, if you enjoyed it,
please leave positive feedback.

About the Author

Thanks for choosing this book, if you enjoyed it, please leave positive feedback.

G.W. Mullins is an Author, Photographer, and Entrepreneur of Native American / Cherokee descent. He has been a published author for over 14 years. His writing has focused on the paranormal and Native American studies.

Mullins has released several books on the history/stories/fables of the Native American Indians. Among his books are the extremely successful "Star People, Sky Gods and Other Tales of the Native American Indians," "Story Teller An Anthology Of Folklore From The Native American Indians," "The Native American Story Book - Stories Of The American Indians For Children Volumes 1-5," "The Native American Cookbook," and "Walking With Spirits Native American Myths, Legends, And Folklore Volumes 1 Thru 6."

He has released the complete series of his Sci/fi Fantasy books "From The Dead Of Night," including the Best-Selling titles – "Daniel Is Waiting" and "Daniel Returns." His most recent work includes the series "Rise Of The Snow Queen" featuring Book One "The Polar Bear King", Book Two "War Of The Witches", and Book Three "The Story of Gerda And Kai."

Mullins' latest releases include two young adult fantasy series, "Rise of the Darklighter" Book One "Dark Awakening," Book Two "Night Of The Demon" and the "Dream Walker" Book Series featuring "Enter the Sandman" and "Wide Awake In Dream Land." Among his other releases are "The Legend Of White Bear (Extended edition)" a Native American paranormal shapeshifting story, "Messages from The Other Side" (a nonfiction book about communication with the dead), and the currently releasing "The Convergence" (a post-apocalyptic book multi-series event).

For further information, on his writing, visit G.W. Mullins' website at *http://gwmullins.wix.com/books*.

<u>Also Available From G.W. Mullins</u>

The Convergence Book Zero Mass Destruction

The Convergence Book One Armageddon

Rise of the Darklighter Book One Dark Awakening

Rise of the Darklighter Book Two Night Of The Demon

Rise Of The Snow Queen Book Three The Story Of Gerda And Kai

Rise Of The Snow Queen Book Two The War Of The Witches

Rise Of The Snow Queen Book One The Polar Bear King

Daniel Awakens A Ghost Story Begins– From The Dead Of Night Prequel

Daniel Is Waiting A Ghost Story – From The Dead Of Night Book One

Daniel Returns A Ghost Story - From The Dead Of Night Book Two

The Frozen Heart

Daniel's Fate A Ghost Story Ends - From The Dead
Of Night Book Four

Dream Walker Book Two Wide Awake In Dream
Land

Dream Walker Book One Enter The Sand Man

Nick Grainger Book One The Curse Of Cleopatra

The Legend Of White Bear (Extended Edition)

Messages From The Other Side Stories of the Dead,
Their Communication, and Unfinished Business

Vengeance – A Paranormal Mystery

Mysteries Of The Unseen World – Ghost,
Hauntings and The Unexplained

Haunted America Stories Of Ghost, Hauntings And
The Unexplained

Timeless – A Paranormal Romance Murder
Mystery

Star People, Sky Gods, And Other Tales Of The
Native American Indians

More Star People, Sky Gods, And Other
Paranormal Tales Of The Native American Indians

Aliens, Gods, and other Paranormal Native
American Tales

Buffalo Tales Of The Native American Indians

Coyote Tales Of The Native American Indians

Bear Tales Of The Native American Indians

Lost Tales Of The Native American Indians Vol 1

Lost Tales Of The Native American Indians Vol 2

Walking With Spirits Native American Myths,
Legends, And Folklore Volumes One Thru Six

The Native American Cookbook

Native American Cooking - An Indian Cookbook
With Legends And Folklore

The Native American Story Book - Stories Of The
American Indians For Children
Volumes One Thru Five

The Best Native American Stories For Children

The Frozen Heart

Cherokee A Collection of American Indian
Legends, Stories And Fables

Creation Myths - Tales Of The Native American
Indians
Strange Tales Of The Native American Indians

Spirit Quest - Stories Of The Native American
Indians

Animal Tales Of The Native American Indians

Medicine Man - Shamanism, Natural Healing,
Remedies And Stories Of The Native American
Indians

Native American Legends: Stories Of The Hopi
Indians Volumes One and Two

Totem Animals Of The Native Americans

The Best Native American Myths, Legends And
Folklore Volumes One Thru Three

Ghosts, Spirits And The Afterlife In Native
American Indian Mythology And Folklore

War Song: Tales Of The Native American Indians

Mullins

For books available from G.W. Mullins in
Hardback, Paperback and eBook

Visit: https://gwmullins.wixsite.com/books

Or scan the QR Code below

Links to G.W. Mullins pages are on Linktree
https://linktr.ee/gw.mullins

From the Author of the Best Selling Novel *Daniel Is Waiting*

Rise of the Snow Queen

Book 1

Sometimes Fairy Tales Don't Have Happy Endings

The Polar Bear King

G.W. Mullins

9 781958 221297